Pat Glendon was a newcomer to Ft. Ellis;
an ex-lawman who wanted to bury his
sensational past and get on with the
business of everyday living.
When Buck Atherton offered a smile and
a helping hand, Glendon accepted. He
knew that the smile masked a remorseless
man with a ready gun.

"Shotgun" Glendon was elected sheriff.
He thought he could tackle both jobs—
clean up Ft. Ellis and keep Atherton
out of town and out of trouble.

But all hell broke loose, because Glendon
didn't figure Atherton would ride into
the hills, challenge his only ally, and
force a reckoning at gunpoint.

LEGEND IN THE DUST

by FRANK O'ROURKE

A SIGNET BOOK

Published by The New American Library

SIGNET TRADEMARK REG. U.S. PAT. OFF. AND FOREIGN COUNTRIES
REGISTERED TRADEMARK—MARCA REGISTRADA
HECHO EN CHICAGO, U.S.A.

SIGNET BOOKS are published by
The New American Library, Inc.,
1301 Avenue of the Americas, New York, New York 10019

FIRST PRINTING, AUGUST, 1968

PRINTED IN THE UNITED STATES OF AMERICA

Chapter One

AT THE TOE of the hills where the evergreens rose in a mass of geometrically precise triangles toward the distant Cristos, the trail was a dusty path winding southward into nowhere. Men had roiled that dust and cattle ranged the swells of those high plains, but only the trail gave lasting evidence of their passage. Offtrail in the rock-cupped hollows beneath the trees around the springs the old fires lay black-ashed and forgotten. Tin cans rusted in shallow-dug litter holes where animals had sniffed and pawed; and the sky above was the only constant color in the land. Deep blue, the sky never changed, but the land effected subtle transformations, greens and browns and reds and yellows shifting seasonally beneath rain and snow, sun and wind, through the circle of time's clock, the unending procession of the years.

The rider came from time's smoky nothingness at dusk, gray-smudged atop the big horse, only hat and horse's ears sharp-etched against the fading amber sky. The rider saw the hollow below the trees, the horse smelled water and sawed gently on the reins.

"All right," Glendon said. "Go on down."

He reined off the trail beside the tank and while the horse drank he knelt and splashed his face and runneled water down his neck. He led the horse into the trees, drove the picket stake deep into the rocky shale, uncinched and slipped the bridle over the rope hackamore. The brown horse shivered with pleasure and went to browsing on the grass that tufted green beneath the trees. While darkness fell Glendon gathered twigs and sticks, lit his fire, and broke open the grub sack. He boiled coffee, cooked bacon and beans, sliced a thick chunk of bread from the staling loaf. He rolled a smoke

5

at meal's end and stood in the full darkness, facing the night wind, tasting the odors of mountain forest and canyon damp. At times he marveled at his own patience. It was not a virtue easily won, much less understood by the owner himself.

He was a thin and slightly stoop-shouldered man whose arms ended in bony wrists and long-fingered hands that forever dangled too far below the finest fitted coat sleeves. His lean hips had filled out some beneath the gun belt, not fat, just fleshed enough to give body to the faded blue levis. His long legs hung spare down the sweat-caked levi tubes, rider's legs of flat muscle lying close around big thigh bones with the knotty calves bulging above his worn boot tops. His black hair, cut long ago by some careless barber, tumbled heavy above his ears and lay thinner on top where the chemical reaction of sun heat beneath the Stetson had worked its toll. His skin was bleached but would never entirely lose brownness, large-pored leathery skin stretched taut over the jutting jaw, around the wide mouth and long nose, tugging shadowed wrinkle sacks beneath his deep-ridged gray eyes. The harsh, rough face held a wealth of experience, of life, but standing lonely in the night with the secret, lost feeling that had sent him down the trail, it was as if he had become one of that breed who, suddenly unsure of their own identity, were at the mercy of all others.

"Fort Ellis," he said aloud. "One more day, horse."

He slept fitfully and rode the trail in a pearl-gray morning that came slowly alive as wind scuffed the clouds away and laid bare the deep blue sky and brassy summer sun. He saw cattle bearing the Cross C brand and, twenty miles to the south, skirted the lake formed by a huge artesian spring that welled upward from the earth's bowels. Below the lake in the bend of the overflow creek he saw the big house, the sheds and shops and corrals. John Colter's Cross C outfit on Big Spring Lake was known far and wide for an open-house policy, for the coffeepot that bubbled on the cookhouse stove. Glendon had not spoken to another man in three days; he entered the yard with his tongue working rustily behind dry lips, tied his horse at the rail, smelled strong coffee and heard voices within the cookhouse. The Cross C slept beneath the cottonwoods in the lazy midday June heat; no one struck up a band to bid him welcome. Everyone was working, only the cripples and the cook would be on tap.

Glendon took the boot-worn stone step through the timbered cookhouse door, raked back his hat and peered into the gloom that was thickened for any man coming from outer sunglare. Sunlight beggared through the windows, weak yellow sop on the dirt floor. The cook turned his shaggy head and spoke in greeting, "Como sta, senor," and brought a clean cup and the gallon coffeepot to the long table; and the only other man in the room glanced upward over his white china cup that smoked thin coffee heat into the viga shadows. That young man was hunched at ease, big legs thrust far beneath the table, levis crotch-wrinkled above his boots. He waved one large hand and smiled at Glendon.

"Set a spell—too damn hot for ridin'."

Glendon sat across the table, stirred in sugar, drank deeply and offered his sigh of thanks. The cook fussed over the stove and Glendon, overly sensitive to the presence of strangers, felt uneasiness in the room. But the young man only grinned sleepily and sipped his coffee.

"Buck," the cook said. "Getting late, no?"

"No," Buck said, and smiled at Glendon. "Riding through?"

"Fort Ellis," Glendon said.

"Not far," Buck said. "An' nothing to see when you get there."

Buck was a squatty young man on first glance. Broad and deep-chested, his rib case was sprung so wide his upper body seemed to descend without curvature into thick legs and large feet. Buck had a cowlick above his round, moon face, his beard was fluffy, his mild blue eyes and straw-colored hair gave him a mussed, innocent appearance. Buck rolled a clumsy smoke, shuffled his feet on the dirt floor, and smiled indolently into his cup. Buck looked harmless but he was wasting time on a ranch noted for long working hours; the fact was bothersome to Glendon, knowing from hearsay how John Colter bossed this outfit.

"Buck," the cook said plaintively. "You go now?"

"Pretty soon," Buck said. "Come down from the north?"

"Yes."

The cook walked soundlessly to the door, glanced up the tree-shaded lane toward the big house, and swung around with a flutter of fat hands. "Buck, the patron is coming!"

"Colter?" Glendon asked.

"Nobody else," Buck smiled. "Ever met him?"

"No."

"Take a good look then," Buck said. "Likely he's wearing a two-bit straw hat, sixty-five-cent hickory shirt, pair of dollar overalls, no socks, brogans that cost all of a buck-fifty. Grand total of three dollars and forty cents, and him worth a million today. Yes sir, take a good look."

"Aih, Buck!" the cook whispered fearfully.

Buck heaved himself erect and gave, in passing, a feeling of sheer laziness, and inability to cope with life, the slow and fusty-headed nature of a dreamer lacking substance. Buck leaned against the wall just inside the door and Glendon saw past him into the bright sunlight and more distant shade of the cottonwood lane; and that was his first view of John Colter coming from the big house, slapping one overall leg with a peeled willow stick, wearing no socks, placing his brogans on the earth with the intent stupid purpose of a plow horse plodding off work toward hay and water.

Shorter than Buck, John Colter was equally solid and strong. Glendon had heard too much about the man to accept the doubtful value of so many stories, but even so his first look made those stories pale. Colter had the face of a cherub and the white hair of Kris Kringle, but the hair faded to dirty yellow as he neared the door, and the rosy face was harsh-wrinkled beneath a wiry three-day beard that failed to hide the sly roughness. Colter, so the saying went, had never been beaten in a deal, a fight, a game of wits. He had ridden into the territory behind ten scrawny cows; now he could not cross his range in one day on a fast horse or count his cattle accurately in a year's time. Glendon saw the legend grow and become lifesize in the door's sunlit frame, the face squinting into the gloom as the voice rasped huskily at the young man.

"By damn, Buck. Ain't you gone yet?"

"Too hot," Buck said affably.

"Hot, my ass," John Colter said. "What we got, company?"

He walked past Buck to the table, and Glendon noticed the absence of belt and gun around the thick waist. Masterson had told him how Colter never wore a gun while bossing fifty men who did, thus taking shrewd advantage of the unwritten law that you did not shoot an unarmed man. Colter carried the peeled willow stick and nothing more; and Buck swung around to watch him with a helpless, admiring look. Colter had increased the tension in the cookhouse; but he simply ignored Buck as he gave Glendon a long, rude look.

"Passing through?"

"Yes."

"Then make yourself to home," Colter said. "What's your name?"

"Pat Glendon."

"Glendon?" Colter tried the sound on his tongue. "Heard

that somewhere. You going to Fort Ellis— Jose, where in hell's your manners, fill up the cups."

Colter broke all the conventions, evidently making his own laws and, more important, making them stick. He rubbed a man the wrong way but under his raspy voice was an edge of humor if a man looked closely and sensed Colter's acid delight in another's discomfort.

Glendon said quietly, "I'm going that way."

"Want a job here?"

"No," he said.

"Well, you bear it in mind. Nothing but pure-quill bastards in Fort Ellis. No place for a decent, law-abiding man. Like Buck here—no place for him in that den of thieves."

"Sure now," Buck said. "I'm strictly law-abiding."

The cook brought a cup for Colter, filled the others, and retreated quickly to the pantry annex. Buck strolled over and sat beside John Colter; and Glendon felt the gap between them. He spoke his thanks to the cook, to Colter, and stepped outside.

Behind him, dulled by the thick adobe walls, their voices rose and fell in argument. Glendon had no business intruding on that private affair. He mounted the brown horse and faced southward where the trail faded hazily into the heat waves.

Buck came suddenly from the cookhouse, walked to the black horse, and mounted. John Colter appeared in the doorway and watched Buck, who sat with one hand on the Winchester stock canted upward beneath his right leg. Buck's face was no longer round and innocent; his head inclined toward Colter like a boar surprised at mast.

"You mind company?" Buck asked.

"Be happy for it," Glendon said.

"Buck," John Colter said gruffly. "Mind now. I don't give you no second chance."

"Thanks for the first," Buck said cheerfully. "Adios."

Glendon nodded good-bye to John Colter and followed Buck from the ranch yard into the trail that arrowed toward Fort Ellis. They traveled a mile in silence before Buck laughed and beat his hat against his thigh, fanning a puff of dust behind.

"Feisty old cuss, eh?"

"Boss trouble?" Glendon asked.

"Oh, I ain't mad at him," Buck said. "But he's sure mad at me. I quit last night."

"Leave him short-handed?"

"Him?" Buck said. "Hell, he's got fifty men on the spread. I just got tired working for wages. Easier ways to make a living."

"Does Colter pay small?"

"Average," Buck said, "but he works you double hard. There's easier ways."

"In this country?" Glendon said.

"Why sure," Buck smiled. "Selling cows to the army for one. You heard of McMann?"

"No."

"He's contractor at Ellis," Buck said. "Supplies the army, buys every cow you can bring him. Work a week, you make more'n Colter pays in a month."

There was a thoroughly likable quality about this Buck, who spoke so openly on touchy subjects to a total stranger. Selling cattle to the army was legitimate business, providing the seller was financially able to purchase cattle and then make his resale through regular channels. But a young man whose sole assets were the clothes on his back, his gun, and his horse, did not possess the cash or the credit. To speak freely of such matters was either stupidity or the nature of a man who went his own free way and cared absolutely nothing for other people. Glendon risked a question that, at other times and places, could bring fast trouble.

"Whose cows, Buck?"

"Whose cows?" Buck said. "Why, John's cows. Nobody else owns any around here."

"You telling me this for fact?" Glendon asked.

"Cross my heart and hope to die."

Glendon had to laugh, and Buck laughed with him. Long ago he'd been this way, filled with an overpowering eagerness for life, the wish for things just beyond his pocketbook; but, remembering, it was not so much the material gains as the need for freedom of the mind. It had brought him close to trouble and death before he whipped that wildness. He could not give advice to Buck, for the young never listen, their ears were tuned to the distant music. But he liked this boy, and he could try. He spoke cautiously.

"You know what that monkey business is called?"

"Oh sure," Buck said.

"No offense?"

"Not a bit," Buck smiled. "You mean well, Pat, but things are different around here. For instance, you see any fences?"

"No."

"Or law?"

"No, unless it's at Fort Ellis."

"You look real good there," Buck said. "Lift up the carpets, peek into the widow's closet. You find any law, you let me know. I been lookin' six months."

"Many of the boys pulling this cow trick?"

"Not more'n thirty," Buck grinned.

"What does Colter say?" he said. "What's he doing about it?"

"I'll sort of draw you a picture," Buck said patiently. "Fort Ellis ain't much of a post any more, just a station to buy beef for the Mescaleros and the other forts to the south. The fort's six miles down from town, both named the same, except the town is all McMann."

"All McMann?"

"Stock and barrel, except for Charley Leslie's store," Buck said happily, "an' Charley don't count for much. McMann's retired army, was a major. He got out a while back and started the town. Having army friends, he sewed up the beef contracts. Him and that colonel at the fort soldiered together, and the colonel don't buy beef from nobody but McMann. That keeps John mad all week and twice as mean on Sundays. But McMann can't buy beef from John 'cause John won't sell him a bull bellow, so McMann has to buy all over and trail his herds in. An' John's got so many cows he can't count 'em, let alone brand 'em all. They just run wild to the west across the river. That sort of clear things up for you, Pat?"

"And no law?" Glendon said wonderingly.

"Bueno," Buck laughed. "Oh, there's a marshal or two hanging around but they don't count. Now I told you enough to hang me, what you figure on doing in Ellis?"

"Buck," he said, "I can't tell you because I don't know myself."

"Just riding loose," Buck said understandingly. "Sure, I savvy how you feel. Passing along, looking around."

"That's it," he said.

"What can you do, Pat?" Buck asked.

"Little of this," he said. "Little of that."

"Foolish question got me a foolish answer," Buck grinned. "But you punched cows, that I know damn well, not lately but sometime."

"Not lately," he admitted; "or ever again."

"Well," Buck said. "You just come along, I'll show you the town. Take a good look—smell too—and make up your mind. When you get tired eating McMann's grub, drinking his whiskey, using his beds, you can always head for El Paso. Now if you was a lawyer, McMann'd give you his own bed. He can't seem to get enough of lawyers."

"But no law?" Glendon said softly.

"It ain't from not trying," Buck said. "I guess he can't find a good lawman. Was it you wore a star someplace, an' showed you could get along with him, then McMann'd give you his bed and his best woman to boot."

"No chance there," Glendon lied.

"No?" Buck said. "Well, too bad."

They rode the trail that followed the dropping roll of land toward the southwest, where a line of trees marked the river as it came from the north and swung in a huge bend toward the panhandle and the hill country and the distant gulf. Glendon wondered how much he had fooled Buck. What was it that left the mark on a man? The faded cloth behind the star, the way a man rode and walked and talked, the way he carried a gun and watched the world around him? Glendon had ridden five hundred miles to leave the star behind, and the first man he spent an hour with—and half a boy at that—seemed to sense, or smell, or feel that past. Then again perhaps he was lucky, for Buck had spoken respectfully in mentioning the law. That meant trust for the moment. If all the past would only shrivel, turn to dust in Kansas, then he would be truly lucky. All he wanted was freedom, a fresh beginning, and it came to him then, riding off the trail into a wagon road formed by many converging paths, that he had silently chided Buck for a young man's dream of freedom when, all the while, his own dreams were far thinner by comparison. Thirty-six years old, hoping wilder hopes than even a boy dared dream.

"Well," Buck said, "there she is."

He looked down the road and saw the brown lumps rising low above the land. That was the town of adobe, part of the land itself; the rains of time could easily dissolve the earth's own. The town was an uncertain being on the face of the land. They came abreast the first shanties that graced the town's soiled skirt, into a single street that fronted the business block and ended at the river bank. Houses were scattered in no order behind the stores, houses built mostly of adobe, bleached by the merciless sun, boasting scraggly shrubs and trees, washlines damp with underwear and trousers and dresses; dozing horses outside the saloon.

Glendon looked twice and counted one saloon. That proved Buck's statement: this town was all McMann. The man's name rang no bell in his memory, but such a man had blood brothers of one size or another from El Paso to Billings. Glendon knew their breed too well.

"Get down," Buck said. "Whisky ain't no good, but it cuts the dust."

"You go on," Glendon said. "I'll get a room."

"Just come along," Buck grinned. "Everything is courtesy of McMann."

Looking up, Glendon noted that the largest building was divided into saloon, hotel, cafe, and store, with glass windows on the second floor above the cafe marking the offices of C. B. Adams, attorney at law, and Sam McMann. Glendon untied his gear and followed Buck across the porch into the saloon; an archway gave off to the hotel lobby and, as Buck shouted greetings to a filled poker table, Glendon passed through to the desk. He signed for a room, dropped his gear, and rejoined Buck at the bar.

"Name it," Buck said. "Don't make no difference what brand you want, you get the same poison."

"Not so," the bartender said primly. "We got two barrels."

"An' one spigot," Buck laughed. "Pat, first round is on me. Then I got to hope you ain't broke 'cause I'm exactly four-bits rich."

"You save that four-bits," Glendon said. "This is my treat."

"Are you goin' to argue?" Buck said.

"I am," he smiled. "Are you breaking up our beautiful friendship?"

Buck laughed and signaled for the glasses. The bartender poured and Glendon drank. He might have tasted worse whisky but he could not remember the place. He swallowed the cough that rose in his throat, held his face rigid as tears pricked his eyes. Buck said, "Come on," and led him back to the poker table and introduced him to six men, a ragtag group with one common characteristic: that narrow-eyed wariness in the presence of a stranger. Buck sat beside a red-haired man and began telling how he'd left the Cross C with old John roaring like a motherless calf. Buck extracted a tableful of mirthless smiles that vanished abruptly as Buck spoke to the red-haired man.

"Ed, when do we start? I'm broke, foot-loose, and eager."

Ed said curtly, "Don't savvy you," and prepared to rise. Buck laughed, the same cheerful sound Glendon had heard in the Cross C cookhouse. His voice boomed above the sound of scraping chairs as he said, "Set down!" and froze them in place. In that moment Glendon read the truth in their faces. The young man who cared nothing for anything or anyone was the strongest here. He laughed and they wanted no part of whatever lay hidden behind his smiling face. Glendon spoke in the silence.

"Private business for you, Buck. See you later."

"Pat, you don't need to go," Buck said. "You won't tell no tales out of school."

"Your friends don't know me," Glendon said. "I'd feel the same way."

"Bueno," Buck said carelessly. "But remember, I ain't showed you around town yet."

He stepped behind Buck's chair and, on impulse, dropped a hand on the thick shoulder. Buck grinned up at him and Glendon understood that quick smile. He had made a friend, whether he wanted the trust or not. Buck was a puppy in many ways, but that was only the outer layer of a young man who had more skins than an onion. Glendon walked from the bar and heard, behind him, the explosive force of Ed's voice, "Who the hell is he, Buck?"

Then Glendon had his gear and took the stairs to the second floor and the last room at hall's end. He stripped and scratched his sweaty flanks in the thick-walled coolness of the room. The management had thoughtfully provided a tin wash basin and one galvanized bucket of water. Glendon took a hand bath, shaved, and put on clean clothes; going back downstairs, he found himself hurrying and that was foolish. He was going nowhere; he had all the time in the world. He stopped at the desk to borrow a handful of matches, and moved onto the porch and looked at the town.

Steps clattered down the stairs between hotel and cafe; a plump little pouter pigeon of a man dressed in blue trousers and a soiled white shirt emerged from the stairwell and stopped beside Glendon, mopping his red face with an equally soiled bandanna. He was slightly frayed around the edges but he had that feeling of the dandy; like heartbeat and breath, vanity died hard in any man, no matter the circumstances.

"Dear God!" he said. "Another scorcher."

"Get much hotter here?" Glendon asked.

"This is only June," the little man said with intense feeling. "In July the hinges melt, in August the devil arrives for his vacation in our fair land. Excuse me for noticing the apparent, but you are new in our town."

"Today," he said.

"My name is Adams," the little man said. "I'm pleased to meet you. In fact, I'm pleased to meet anyone new in Fort Ellis."

"Glendon," he said.

Adams had a sharp handclasp and sharper eyes that examined Glendon while he lit a cigar and teetered on his heels. "Will you join me in something cool?"

"No thanks," Glendon said.

"I know that tone of disgust," Adams said. "You've sampled the whisky and you refuse to be twice-burned. I don't blame you. I referred to root beer in the cafe. I keep my own bottle in my rooms. I may live a trifle longer that way. . . . Just passing through, Mr. Glendon?"

"Looking around," he said. "Is there a livery barn handy?"

"Right down the street," Adams said. "This side. I recommend it highly."

"I'll try that root beer another time," Glendon said politely. "My horse needs shade."

He stepped off the porch and led the brown horse fifty steps to a cavernous barn that promised both shade and coolness. The hostler led the brown horse into the shadowy alleyway depths and Glendon stood in the door shade, encompassing all of Fort Ellis in one glance. Across from McMann's buildings was another store—Leslie's, by the sign—and the post office and a barbershop with its rickety candy-striped pole. Abutting the livery barn was a harness and saddle shop; and those buildings represented the total business in Fort Ellis.

Glendon walked away from the shabbiness and the heat, between scattered houses, past a dog that barked without animosity from the prickly shelter of a rose bush. He came to the riverbank and descended the cutbank grade scraped out by fresno and team, and turned north along the river under the cottonwoods that formed their umbrellas over the lower willows. Water snored and grunted beneath the bank, a thin stream no more than thirty yards wide.

He rolled a cigaret and flipped his match upstream into the dark current; and saw the red bobber below an overhanging willow branch that touched water and formed a silent fan of ripples. The line rose from bobber to a willow pole, and the pole was held by a fisherman sitting on a rock, head now turned from the water, watching him in silent amusement. Glendon removed his hat. He was an intruder, frightening the fish. He began a retreat but the fisherman said, "No luck anyway. Guess it's too hot today."

There was no resentment in her voice. Glendon paused gratefully and found old memories of his youth along the Elkhorn, fishing trotlines with cornballs and chicken guts, coming in early dawn to haul the line, count the night's catch of bullheads and catfish, then sit with a willow pole and bobber, hoping for more cat and mostly catching carp. A long time ago, in another world gone forever; the man would never recapture the boy he had been.

"How deep is it?" he asked.

"About five feet," she said. "Deeper under the cutbanks. I'm using worms."

"What do you catch here?" he asked.

"Rainbows and browns," she said. "I'm worm fishing for trout, and that's a mortal sin. Trouble is, no matter what bait I use, I catch suckers."

"I grew up that way," Glendon said. "Willow pole and a can of worms."

"Catfish?"

"And bullheads," he said. "Carp, suckers, sunfish."

"In Kansas?"

"Nebraska," Glendon said. "The Elkhorn, the Platte, the Niobrara."

"I fished the Republican," she said. "But that was a long time ago."

She had a narrow, oval face crowned with a thick head of chestnut hair that shimmered when leaf-let sunlight trembled downward through the cottonwoods. Her forehead was high, her eyes brown, her nose quite long with a cartilage bump on the vaguely arrogant bridge. Her mouth was full and wide, her chin well set and stubborn above the browned V of her man's blue shirt and slender, rounded body. She wore levis and boots, and the chestnut hair was pinned behind her ears in two fat braids. Her face was sober and plain until she smiled at her own words; then it came alive with interest as she said, "You're new in town?"

"Yes," he said. "Sorry I bothered you."

"No bother," she said. "You've stirred up a dull day."

"Why is that?" Glendon asked.

"Not a man in town fishes here," she said, "let alone comes down. I doubt they know a fish from a sausage. You'll be a marked man from the word go. Very suspicious."

He saw the glint of laughter and smiled in return. He replaced his hat, touched it respectfully, and went away to the road. A strange town, housing people of Buck's kind, lawyers like C. B. Adams, and the unseen McMann. Not to mention this woman in man's clothing fishing on a hot afternoon, undisturbed by his invasion of her privacy. Her action was made stranger when he remembered the gold wedding band on her left hand; it took a different sort of woman to go fishing with a house and family depending on her guiding hand. Glendon came once more to the livery barn and paused in the welcome shade to look again at the town and pull his ragged thoughts together.

He had left Kansas two weeks ago with a headful of plans. A man always had plans; from those ideas came all of life. But a man could not worship those ideas blindly; he used them as they came, like shirts, and put the best of each into his life. The point in question, it seemed, was whether he would ever have a worthwhile idea, find a spot on earth that seemed to fill his needs. He had to stop somewhere, if only for a little while, and face the truth: he had nothing before him. But if all a man faced was nothingness, if all he had done in the past came down to that dismal present, then a man had to fight against nothingness itself. Glendon wiped the fresh sweat from his face; this was as good as any place on earth to rest and plan.

Swift Stamm was twenty-seven years old, her first name a legacy from the grandfather on her mother's side who insisted his daughter's firstborn bear his name. Her sex did not change the adamant old man; and all things being equal, her name was far better than many around her, attached to various long-suffering girls for life. The name, like a good shoe, seemed to fit more comfortably with the passing years. She was a tomboy, her mother's despair, for even in young womanhood she preferred pants and shirts instead of long-flowing dresses that choked not only a woman's body but her very thoughts.

Swift Stamm married a young lawyer at the age of nineteen; it was necessary, according to the neighbors, but of which specific necessity they chose not to elaborate, only to insinuate. Her true reason was loneliness that followed the flu epidemic and the death of her parents; and Bill Stamm had grown up across the backyard fence, gone off to college, and come home to renew his easy friendship with the coltish girl now become a woman. For her it was not the love young women expect; it was necessity. For Bill Stamm it was the nature of the times and a lack of more eligible girls. Bill Stamm was a pleasant young fellow then; but age changes all men. They did very well for five years but lawyering in that Kansas town forced a man to cultivate business over the bar. Bill Stamm's body was weaker than his mind. He developed a cough, they moved westward and came eventually to Fort Ellis, where Bill Stamm became junior member of the C. B. Adams law firm.

Two years ago Bill Stamm had taken one drink too many and laid his thick, harsh tongue on the wrong man. They brought the sad news to Swift; now she lived on in Fort Ellis, doing bookwork for Adams and McMann, living alone and evidently enjoying the view. She had few friends among the stiffer necks, but she was well-liked by children and older people. She spent a good many hours fishing, riding out along the river, reading books and tending her garden. She wore dresses when necessary but refused to cramp her feet in those abominations tenderly described as ladies' shoes, those needle-toed, high-heeled monstrosities. She wore boots and sandals, and allowed her fine, clear skin to burn dark as a paisano's in the summer.

Her personal reputation was above reproach; therefore, the few good ladies in and around Fort Ellis resentfully ripped it to ribbons. They were the people who thought a house with the proper wife and children, the proper business and church and neighbors and all the nice things, all the trappings—all these were all of life. But life at best was a savage business, like the people it served, hard and cold and only sweet to the strong. Swift did not care; she worked for Adams and McMann, she lived her independent life and bowed to no one in her principles, which, as with all people who possessed real principles, were not worn on her sleeve.

She watched the stranger walk from sight and wondered at his gentleness; and odder, had a feeling of shared loneliness, her own recurrent sensation of sitting helpless on the treadmill of time. She wound her line around the willow pole and stuck the hook into the bobber. She walked the hot road to her small house a hundred yards behind the business block, and passed through the arbor gate into her private world. Bill Stamm had bought the house from McMann four years ago. She had planted roses around the foundations, started an osage-orange hedge inside the wall; two cottonwood trees in the backyard shaded her garden and gave her one small spot in which she could isolate herself from the town. The barrier was mostly in her mind, as all barriers were, for walls gave no true isolation. Thoughts and memories and dreams had the bad habit of piercing all barriers.

She set the fishing pole against the porch rail and entered

the house that offered coolness, if nothing more. She changed into sandals and a cotton dress, gave her braids a tug, and went unhurriedly across the back lot to the hotel. She had an hour's work on Adams' books; and McMann had undoubtedly discovered something new since dinnertime. She traveled the narrow alley between the cafe and store walls, swung onto the boardwalk, and found McMann and Adams on the hotel porch, smoking those vile cigars, masters of all they surveyed. She knew them so well; too well, in fact, for comfort.

McMann was in his late fifties, very much the retired major of cavalry, complete with short wiry hair, ruffish mustache, round stomach held erect like a shield, stubby legs plunged into fine black boots; and those straight military shoulders held firmly in line. McMann wore black and gray suits with white broadcloth shirts and black string bow ties, his vest crossed with a gold chain holding the Elgin repeater and lodge pin. His army ring glinted on his left fourth finger, too deeply embedded in the fat creases ever to be removed in life; and while he carried no visible arms Swift Stamm was familiar with the hip-pocket holster and the bulldog .38 hidden beneath his coattails.

McMann faced the world smugly from stern features that matched the set of his shoulders, his face highlighted by the cropped sandy hair and mustache, with tiny crabapple spots of red fattening the curves of his cheeks. His eyes were sharp blue, his teeth lay yellowish behind thin red lips, his jaw was a block of granite above his thick neck. McMann gave absolute pause to the legend that old soldiers just fade away; he gave, instead, the feeling that he might never die, that age was only a minor irritant in his path through immortal life. McMann walked in military fashion, short arms swinging precisely at his sides. He rode in the same way and he spoke in only one tone—the brusque, clipped words of a man accustomed to giving orders and expecting no arguments. Yet, by the very nature of his business in Fort Ellis, he received and absorbed a plethora of such talk from men who had no appreciation, let alone awe, for the military. With those men McMann swallowed his fury and argued fluently in Spanish or English, plus a third language composed of free-swinging Elizabethan profanity that did more to control his rough colleagues than all the studied arguments in the world. He never failed to capitalize on this talent when other methods failed.

McMann had built his empire on simple cornerstones: his

army career, which gave him invaluable connections; and his unquestioned power in Fort Ellis, which, combined with cash and the legal might of C. B. Adams, enabled him to back up his desires. Few men had needed more in history. McMann was strong enough to succeed with either one of the two; and having both, he was, at the moment, unbeatable. Even John Colter could not dent McMann's position, and John Colter was cut from the same monolithic granite.

Swift Stamm knew all this, and more, as she gave her employers a wave and turned up the stairway between cafe and hotel. She passed from view and McMann, having doffed his hat, resumed his conversation with C. B. Adams. McMann had been upstairs a few minutes earlier, watching Glendon enter the hotel; now he mused on the name.

"Glendon—the name is vaguely familiar."

"I'll have his luggage inspected," Adams said.

"Use Felipe," McMann said. "But we'll find nothing. If he is official, his breed is too smart for that."

"We can try," Adams said. "Have you seen Ed and young Buck?"

"Not yet."

"Buck quit Cross C last night," Adams said.

"By God!" McMann smiled. "I wonder how old John took that alum pill."

"If I were Colter," Adams said, "I'd never have allowed Buck to leave Cross C alive."

"Hogwash," McMann said. "He's just another reckless young fool. I know, he's killed three men. That makes him stupid plus reckless, ideal for our purpose. But not that bad. Ed's the best of the bunch."

"You truly think so?" Adams asked.

"Compare their records," McMann said. "As you might phrase it, counselor, Ed has precedent going in his favor."

"Sam," Adams said quietly, "that boy in there is a cyclone, a tornado. He doesn't know it yet, you don't, no one seems to smell the danger in that boy. But I do. And why? Because it is my business to read people."

"And what do you read?" McMann said tolerantly. "Give me one of your special pleas, counselor."

"Buck fits something I learned long ago," Adams said. "Something I discussed at length with a brilliant man. We talked one night—"

"Over how many bottles?"

"One or two," Adams said stiffly. "It doesn't matter. You see, I remember this. We talked of life. How we never knew what begins the life cycle of anything, animals, plants, humans. But we know that each little act of that cycle is a preparation for the next. And should the animal, the plant, the human miss one clue, it dies. The getting-ready mechanism is an odd and fearsome thing, Sam. We see the light flicker and our eyes blink, we hear a dangerous sound and our glands shoot courage into our blood. Sam, all living is action and human life is action with thought, with the brain working, action directed toward the future, having a purpose. Today's action has a bearing on tomorrow. And every living action is an act of choice. Note that, Sam, an act of choice."

"Get to the point," McMann said impatiently.

"The point," Adams said, "is that Buck is a human with thoughtful action. Now, living action being an act of choice, it would surely be true that Buck has made his choice in life. But Buck's action has no thought for the future. I say that Buck is a throwback, an atavism, concerned only with the moment, thinking not at all of the future or the results and the terrors his acts might bring down not only for those directly concerned but for himself and the innocent as well. Sam, the boy is dangerous. My advice to you is, treat him politely but send him on his way. Get him out of this country. He is like the powder keg behind the stove, Sam. Don't start a fire and put your best cake in the oven."

McMann threw his cigar into the street. He had listened closely, as he did always to Adams, and as always concealed his resultant opinions. He said, "It is a thought," and went through the hotel lobby and down the back hall to a large, bare room facing upon the rubbish-choked yard. A narrow door opened into the saloon's storage room; it made possible a highly desired privacy for certain meetings. Waiting for Buck and Ed Bailey, McMann fingered a fresh cigar.

The door opened; Ed Bailey led Buck inside and both sank gingerly into the chairs across the battered table. McMann studied Buck while lighting, drawing, and expelling cigar smoke. He saw a young lout—for all slouchy men were louts in the mirror of McMann's own military mind—willing to do anything for money. McMann dropped his match and grunted away Adams' fears.

"You," he said. "Quit the Cross C, eh?"

"Last night," Buck said lazily. "Figure on taking some of that easy money from you."

McMann said curtly, "You are too brash and outspoken. Let's understand that now and hereafter."

Buck turned sleepily to Ed Bailey. "Cut up that Greek for me, Ed. I don't savvy nothin' but American and Mex."

Ed Bailey was in the awkward middle, forced to reduce McMann's blood pressure, knowing that McMann's next move was a stream of his explosive profanity; and knowing all too well how Buck would react. Bailey said hastily, "Sometimes I don't savvy the major myself, Buck, but he sure means well. He's saying that shut mouths are good business. That right, Major?"

"Yes," McMann said. "Just so Buck understands."

"Oh, I savvy," Buck smiled. "You want some more Cross C cows."

McMann swallowed his choler and faced up to the tools at hand: good, bad, or indifferent, he could find no better men. He spoke distinctly, "I will be in the market for five hundred head two weeks from today."

"What price, Major?" Ed Bailey asked.

"The same," McMann said. "Delivery at my pens across the river."

"Bueno," Ed Bailey said. "Come on, Buck. Let's have one last drink and get to work."

McMann did not allow himself a move until the connecting doors closed; then he brought one flat hand down viciously. Dangerous? He wondered if Colter had deliberately foisted Buck off on him; if so, old John was probably laughing fit to kill. Buck had killed three men! Buck scared all the others of his stripe! McMann snorted. The young fool was apt to trip over his own feet and break his neck before he roped a single cow.

Glendon lay on his lumpy mattress in the early dusk and examined his puzzled thoughts once more. If a man could only find what was common to all men, he might discover the whole truth of man's lost brotherhood; and finding that, find himself. Then he could match the place to live with the blessing of peace. Evidently that Utopian place existed only in the soul—but Glendon had begun to doubt the presence of a soul, whatever it was supposed to be, wherever it was supposed to lie within a man. And soul-searching was a waste of time if a man lacked the prime requisite: true understanding of himself. He had come from the river and dozed until now, at dusk, his stomach proved more sensible than his thoughts. He dreamed hopefully about the right place on earth, and his stomach called a practical halt.

Glendon washed his face and took the stairs. He was only

splitting the eternal hairs of every man's dilemma; his mind was already made up. He had decided to stay a while the moment he turned from the river.

He passed through the lobby into the cafe and ate his meal at the rear table. C. B. Adams found him there and plumped down wearily.

"Root beer," Adams told the waitress, "and be generous with the ice, Rosie." Then he rubbed his chin and smiled. "The heat gets me."

"Try coffee," Glendon said.

"I know," Adams said. "Doctors maintain it extrudes the sweats and poisons, keeps you cooler. No matter, I'll drink root beer and burn inwardly. Well, what have you decided about our fair city?"

"I'd stay a while," Glendon said, "if I could rent a place."

Adams erected a finger steeple of momentary thought. The waitress brought his drink and Adams stared at the straw chaff floating on the dark brown liquid. He said, "Four houses available, one decent. North of here toward the river. Dirty, unfurnished, no window glass, the well needs cleaning. A shed for your horse, a backyard."

"And the owner?"

"Major McMann," Adams smiled. "I represent him, and I'll not argue rent. You name a figure, I'm apt to snap you up."

Half-joking, Glendon said, "How about five dollars?"

"Taken," Adams said. "A ridiculous price, of course, but the house itself is ridiculous. If you have the courage to clean and furnish it, five dollars a month is sufficient. . . . Are you thinking of staying on permanently?"

"I can't say," Glendon said. "What time will you be up tomorrow?"

"Eight," Adams said. "Meet me at breakfast."

"What about supplies?"

"You have two stores," Adams said. "The major's, and Mr. Leslie's across the street."

Glendon said quietly, "There's a choice in Fort Ellis?"

"There is always a choice," Adams said. "It is only the result of final choice that proves a man's sagacity."

"I buy where the price is right," Glendon said. "Good-night."

He paid his tab and went outside to the south end of the porch and smoked a cigar in the deepening night. The hitch rails were deserted, the saloon was quiet for such an early hour. Buck and his friends had departed while Glendon took a siesta. That was the way of it for a man in a strange town; the night hours dragged when he had nothing to occupy mind and body. Glendon dropped his cigar and turned through the lobby to the stairs. He hoped one of the stores had fish line and bobbers and hooks.

Chapter Two

CHARLEY LESLIE entered his general store and prowled the aisles, pussy-footing around his janitor's damp mop strokes. He concluded his inspection at the front window, through which he saw the stranger just opening McMann's store door. Charley Leslie had his own grapevine that, last night, had brought him news of Glendon's arrival. If Glendon was another McMann import he would not bother to cross the street; if he was a loner truly interested in low prices he'd come visiting shortly. Charley Leslie massaged his clean-shaven jaw and waited patiently.

He was a handsome man with stiff, austere features rigidly cast beneath smooth black hair. The long nose dominated his friar's face, the mouth passing unnoticed until it moved in flexible, thin-lipped agility and spoke in his clear, cold voice. He had slipped into town six months ago, bought the vacant building from McMann's bankrupt competitor, laid in an excellent stock, and squared off for battle in the commercial ring. McMann had learned absolutely nothing about his past, beginning with the opening gambit that backfired. Swift Stamm, coming over to purchase needles, had told him frankly that she worked for McMann.

"What does the major wish to know?" Leslie had asked.

"How long can you last," Swift said, "once he starts cutting prices?"

"As long as he can," Charley Leslie smiled. "Tell him I relish competition."

She had laughed with him, and they got along famously. He was on a dangerous job and dared not make mistakes, yet he did. Knowing that John Colter hated everyone connected with McMann, Leslie had fallen in love. In his own chilly fashion he tried to express those tender sentiments but, beyond pleasant friendship, Swift gave him no encouragement.

So life had rolled along for six months, McMann had cut prices, learned that Leslie could not be broken, and raised prices to the old level. Thereafter Charley Leslie made a firm practice of underbidding McMann's store on every item. He became friendly with C. B. Adams and enjoyed many a good argument in the cafe; and he gained McMann's grudging respect by pandering cleverly to the major's vanity. He addressed McMann by the military title, he asked questions about battles and tactics and famous generals, he built up their interest in him while doing his own job in perfect style. As for Swift, his own cynicism made him recognize his worth to her: he was the only man in town worthy of her time.

He thought of her now as Glendon crossed the street and entered his store. Charley Leslie introduced himself, shook hands, and followed Glendon around the aisles, jotting down each item mentioned, learning that Glendon's house would be cleaned by noon and he wanted to move in at once. Charley Leslie stepped behind his front counter, finished checking prices, and quoted each article a bit under McMann's rates.

"You're cheaper," Glendon said.

"I make a fair profit," Leslie said mildly. "I am not in business to fleece my customers."

"I'll take the lot," Glendon said. "Can you haul it over early this afternoon?"

"Yes," Leslie said. "Now, is there anything else?"

"Have you got fishing tackle?"

"A small stock."

"I want line, bobbers, sinkers, hooks."

Charley Leslie smiled. "I don't believe it."

"What?"

"Another fisherman," Leslie said. "I never thought it would happen in Fort Ellis."

Leslie saw the faint glint of laughter glow and fade in Glendon's eyes. He could not fathom that humor but he had struck a responsive spark, and that was good enough on first meeting. It gave him a clue to Glendon's character; and one clue was often sufficient.

Glendon said, "Are you the other one?"

"No," Leslie said. "Swift Stamm is our fisherman. She never gives up but she catches fewer fish than anyone I know."

"Catching is the least of it," Glendon said. "What's the total damage?"

Leslie added the total, accepted cash, and made the small change. Glendon departed as quietly as he came, and Leslie went straight to the warehouse loading dock and handed the list to Manuel, who waited for the important words.

"Deliver this," Leslie said. "Then go on out. Tell Colter that Glendon is not McMann's boy. Ed Bailey took Buck and that crew upriver yesterday, which means trouble in the hills. Nothing else at present except we needn't worry about Glendon."

"No?"

"He's not looking for trouble," Leslie said. "He's a fisherman."

"He would not dodge it," Manuel said. "He has that look."

"What look?" Leslie said impatiently. "You're always judging a man by his look. The face tells nothing."

"He has it," Manuel said doggedly. "Adios, senor."

Leslie stood alone after Manuel had gone, reviewing his own opinion of Glendon. Swift was a fisherman and Glendon betrayed the same habit; and the trait showed a certain facet of character: such a person wanted no part of violence. They wanted the life that went with willow poles and bobbers, the placid day-by-day existence of three meals, a clean bed, and no enemies shooting through lamplit windows. Glendon was a failure searching for success, forever finding nothing, forever going on.

Oh, yes? Charley Leslie thought, and what of himself? Was he any better?

How much longer would Colter play this silly game? Bringing him down here from the north, backing him in the store, asking nothing more vital than belated information on McMann's actions. Not even caring that cattle were stolen regularly as the sun rose, just receiving Manuel's skimpy facts and doing nothing. Six months of it had shortened Leslie's temper and sharpened his appetite for big money. He was not making it in the store, his sole source of income as agreed upon when Colter made the deal, and he did not intend to endure the stalemate much longer. If Colter made no definite move within two months, he would try a deal with McMann or leave the country.

Charley Leslie wheeled through the store and crossed over to the cafe. He sat beside Adams, ordered coffee, and offered his cigar case. Adams sniffed and accepted.

"How do you keep them so fresh, Charley?"

"Cork-lined humidor," Leslie said. "Slice of apple. Who are you skinning these days, C. B.?"

"We just lost a cash customer," Adams said. "My employer is planning your demise."

"Bullet or knife?" Leslie asked.

"Boiling in oil," Adams grinned. Having completed their usual exchange, Adams lit his cigar and turned on the stool. "Charley, you've done pretty well but have you thought how much better you'd do if you joined us?"

"I have," Leslie said.

"Then give us a chance," Adams said. "Let's have a serious talk one of these days."

"I'll keep it in mind," Leslie said. He dropped a dime on the counter. "Swift upstairs?"

"Busy," Adams said. "I'll convey all messages."

"I'm going riding after supper," Leslie said. "Tell her I'll stop by."

He left the cafe and crossed to his store, hiding his elation behind the long-nosed, expressionless face. Adams had finally made the first move. Now it was Colter's turn; and Colter had better move fast.

Leslie closed the door behind him; and in the cafe, trouser seat clinging stickily to the stool, C. B. Adams smiled. Leslie had nibbled at the bait; another month and they'd have him in the fold. Adams pulled his trousers loose and hurried upstairs to tell McMann the good news.

The house was clean, the furniture was installed, the shelves were stocked with food. Glendon started a fire in the cookstove, boiled coffee, and drank in reflective silence, standing in the back door that faced the river. He rinsed the cup, took up the shining new shovel, and went hunting in the earth beneath the osage hedge. He spaded a few scrawny worms, gathered his tackle, and walked to the river. Remembering Swift Stamm, he moved a hundred yards upstream from her favorite spot in respect for her privacy, wanting the same for himself. He cut a willow pole, tied on his line, and baited up. The bobber splashed when he threw out, and then he didn't care if the fish took his worm or swam free. He butted the pole deep into the bank and stripped off his clothes.

He spent half an hour in waist-deep water at the upper end of the hole, washing and floating, heels dug into the bottom sand against current tug, spreading his fingers lax upon the surface. Cool and lazy in late afternoon, he slipped on his pants and sat beside the pole, gazing across the river toward the distant peaks. He saw nothing and everything in that moment, thinking only how fine it was to drowse through a summer day. He had worked forever, it seemed, just for this.

He had eleven hundred dollars in cash, life-savings of thirty-six years, enough to bring him through the summer and take him further down the road come fall. Something would turn up then; it always did for a man who taught himself the lesson Glendon was learning with such agonizing slowness: to stop pressing luck, let life lead the way. Glendon lay back and closed his eyes; the river gurgled at his feet and the sky darkened as a tiny wind came up. And this time she spoke first, having walked soundlessly upstream from her customary spot.

"Thought I'd find you here."

Glendon scrambled to a sitting position and rubbed both hands self-consciously across his bare chest. He reached for his shirt and she said, "Leave it off if it's cooler," and sat nearby, pole slanting between her trousered legs. "Any luck?"

"No," Glendon said. "I was too busy swimming."

"Take a look."

He pulled his line and saw the bare hook, the sinker spinning lazily above the hookeye. She grinned and Glendon smiled with her and at himself.

"They do that," she said. "Steal you blind, Mr. Glendon."

"Miss Stamm," he said. "Is that correct?"

"Mrs. Stamm," she said. "Charley told me you stopped by."

"Mrs. Stamm?"

"In name only. I'm a widow, Mr. Glendon."

She explained casually and he considered her words while buttoning his shirt and slapping his hat against his leg. She wore the wedding ring but the widow part explained a good deal—the fishing and the feeling of independence she gave him. He searched for words and found nothing suitable, and once more had the feeling that she did not give a tinker's damn about false sentiment or equally false words used solely to fill an awkward breech.

"You picked a good house," she said. "Did Maria clean it?"

"You can eat off the floor," Glendon said.

"I'm your neighbor," she said. "The house just south of you, the one with the big cottonwoods."

He said, "That's fine," and wondered why he spoke the banal words. He rose and wrapped his line and gave his hat a tug. "Getting late," he said, and when he turned from the river she walked easily beside him. He touched his hat, preparatory to wishing her good-night, but she pointed her pole toward the cottonwoods and said, "Come in for coffee, Mr. Glendon. You can't have a housewarming so let's do the next best thing."

"Thank you," Glendon said. "I hope—"

"Neighbors?" she asked. "You're my neighbor now. Are you turning down my offer?"

"No," Glendon said. "If you don't care about the neighbors, why, I'll tell you the truth—I never gave a damn what they thought."

"That's why I invited you," she smiled. "I never gave a damn either. Come in."

He followed her through a back gate, around the garden plot, into the small kitchen that gleamed from white-washed walls when she lit the lamp and trimmed the wick. She put coffee on and brought cups, sliced a yellow pound cake, set out a dish of dried apricots, poured the coffee and sat across the table, talking all the while about the heat and the town and the fact she hoped he was hungry because cake dried out so fast in this country. Then, over her cup, she said soberly, "I work for McMann and Adams, Mr. Glendon. I thought you should know that."

"Why?" he said. "Is it a sin?"

"Because you are a stranger in town," she said, "and I always receive orders from the major to cross-examine every stranger."

"That's why you invited me in?" he asked.

"No," she smiled. "I never obey the major's orders. He knows it, but he keeps trying. You like to fish and that's enough reason to know you. Fort Ellis is a dull town, Mr. Glendon, and Charley Leslie is the only other person I can talk with. I am sounding you out for the major, and I am not. Do you understand?"

"Yes," Glendon said. "It wasn't necessary to explain."

"It was," she said. "You'll soon get acquainted, you'll hear from others that I'm the major's spy. I'd rather tell you myself. Then too, you can't sit a rail here. You're either for the major or against him. If you're against him, then you'll be moving on as soon as he gets around to you."

"Even if I have no axe to grind?" Glendon said.

"The major will give you an axe," she said. "Then he'll grind it. . . . When were you last in Kansas?"

And suddenly he realized that she was lonely, that she needed someone who saw, with her, the country where her memories were buried. Good or bad, it was always a blessing to have someone who shared those memories, even a stranger. Well, he was not exactly a stranger to her now, because he did know Kansas. And he could tell her a few things about being lonely in a crowd.

He ate half his slice of cake and said quietly, "When was I last in Kansas? About three weeks ago."

"How is it this year along the Republican?" she asked.

"Back there?" Glendon said. "Mighty good. . . . Thank you, I believe I will have another slice."

Twenty miles west of the river and thirty miles north of Fort Ellis, Buck lay beside the cookfire and listened to Ed Bailey pair the boys off for tomorrow. It would be a rough, killing time but nothing a man couldn't take cheerfully, running down five hundred head of Colter's cattle. Then a leisurely drive south to McMann's pens, the payoff in cash, and a month of fun. Buck grinned sleepily at the fire. They'd patronize McMann a couple of days, just for looks, and ride north to Sherman where nobody asked questions and a dance was held every Saturday night come rain or shine.

"Ed," Buck said. "Let's go up to Sherman, eh?"

"Fandango?"

"I was there once," Buck said. "Met a nice little girl."

"Mex?"

"Sure," Buck said, "an' she gave me the eye. I ought to return the favor."

"She married?"

"Guess so," Buck said. "It don't matter."

"You watch that," Ed Bailey said. "A knife in the dark ain't no laughing matter."

"You're an old maid," Buck said amiably. "Stop worrying. How many head can we gather tomorrow?"

"Enough," Ed Bailey said. "You and me are taking the big canyon, the others'll circle out and drive into us. We'll sweat, brother, but the payoff's worth the time. Let's hit the straw. Long day comin'."

Buck lay back and watched the stars. He thought ahead to the payoff, the dance, and that girl. But no further. He hoped Glendon had stayed in Fort Ellis; maybe he could persuade Pat to come along to Sherman. Then Buck thought of John Colter and laughed softly. Old John was sure a case. Everybody afraid of him, and why? You couldn't lose more than life itself, and you might as well spend life as it came. Buck gave no thought to the future, to the dreams he might twist into reality, to the trouble that clung to him like steel to a

magnet. Once in a while Ed Bailey, or someone, got to
talking about a man's soul and how he ought to make peace
with it while he had time; but that sort of thinking was
something Buck gave little time to. He had known a lot of
men who bragged about their souls and proved themselves
worse off in the end for claiming something they couldn't
hold in their hand.

The summer wore on and the heat increased. Glendon
lived a quiet life that circumscribed no more than grocery
shopping and fishing along the river, his only companions
Swift Stamm and, occasionally, cafe talk with C. B. Adams.
As the heat rose Glendon spent more time on the river. Swift
was there, too, and they talked together under the cottonwoods and walked homeward to have coffee and talk some
more. Glendon spoke only when she offered him the chance,
and they got along fine talking of Kansas and other places,
but Swift was a good deal like himself. She treasured solitude.

Glendon slept late and ate small, fished the river, watched
the mercury climb as June shriveled its string. Two weeks
after Buck left town, Glendon looked up from his bobber
and saw a dust snake coming down from the hills across the
river; an hour later he counted the trail herd as it wound into
McMann's pens. McMann and Adams crossed over a few
minutes later and met with the riders in haystack shade; a
close group of grimy, unshaven men who whooped and
laughed as they left the paymasters and headed for town.
Fresh money burning a hole in their pockets, Glendon
thought. Fort Ellis would come jarringly awake tonight.

He looked down at the water and gave his pole a twitch.
The dust and the cattle and their distant talk, the world of
men doing something, no matter if good or bad, destroyed
his solitude. He wrapped his line and walked home, curious
about those cattle in the river pens.

He wondered if they were branded, or clean, or if the long
iron had worked them over; he wondered how many days
they would stay in full view of all the world. It seemed
incredible that Colter allowed such open theft; further north
such bald-faced rustling would start a war bigger than any
banana-republic revolution. Glendon ate a cold supper,
shaved his sun-browned face, and walked uptown. He barely
cleared the saloon doors when Buck came shouting from the
bar to squeeze him in a sweaty bearhug and yell happily,
"Heard you stayed. Come on now, Pat. My turn to buy."

"One drink," Glendon said. "It's good to see you, Buck."

"Good to see you," Buck grinned. "Pat, what you been doin'?"

"Loafing," he said. "Just plain loafing."

"An' us working like dogs," Buck said. "But we sure got paid for our trouble. Listen, we're going upriver in a couple days. Want to come along?"

"Where to?" he asked.

"Sherman," Buck said. "There's a saloon with GOOD whisky, an' girls, an' a dance on Saturday night."

"Can't be gone too long," he said. "Got to water my garden."

"Garden," Buck said. "What you planted?"

"Lettuce and peas," Glendon said. "And some hope."

He spoke his inner thoughts and Buck smiled without understanding, not really listening, living for the moment and the sounds around them. "Hell," Buck said. "It ain't far to Sherman. Ride along, see the country."

"I'll let you know tomorrow," he said. "Go back to that poker game."

"You play?" Buck asked innocently.

"I play some," Glendon said, "but not tonight. You gouge your friends first."

He gave Buck a slap and pushed him toward the table where Ed Bailey sat shuffling cards, watching them moodily. They hadn't shaved or washed yet, they were drinking and reaching out for their fun in sweat-grimed clothes, in dusty beards and leather-cracked boots. It went that way for men who worked so hard that time was quicksilver between their fingers, slipping from them faster than they reached. Glendon went through the hotel to the cafe, ordered coffee, and tried a sweet roll. He was hunched over his cup, anticipating night's first coolness, when he heard the shot.

"And here we go again," the waitress said cynically.

Glendon rose without volition, an old war horse responding to conditioned reflexes. He checked his advance midway through the hotel lobby, walked slowly behind the rush to the saloon where men were crowded in a thick circle facing the bar. Boots drummed on the porch boards and burst inside with a sharp command from the owner, "Stand back!" All those crowding men opened ranks, some spilling backward against Glendon. One was Joe Jones, the night man at the livery barn.

"What happened?" Glendon asked.

"Buck," Jones said. "Some damned fool got drunk and sassy."

"Dead?"

"You heard one shot, didn't you?"

"Yes," he said.

"That's all Buck ever takes. Sure he's dead and here's the major raising hell!"

Glendon had lived two weeks in Fort Ellis and failed to meet McMann. He had seen the major on the street and riding past, but never in action. Curiosity made him edge into the saloon and along the wall until he had a clear view of the scene. He saw the dead man on the floor, sprawled beside a bar spittoon and a broken glass. Buck stood at the end of the bar, elbows on the knurled rail, and McMann had marched forward midway between the body and Buck. C. B. Adams came bustling inside at that moment, skipped around the body, and stood alertly beside McMann.

"Well," McMann said curtly. "What happened?"

"He up and started trouble," Buck said. "I had to take him."

"Prince?"

"Yessir, Major?" the prim bartender said.

"Is that true?"

"Yessir," Prince said. "Nothing else Buck could do. This feller was drunk and mean, he just started cussing Buck and went for his gun."

"Self-defense?" McMann said.

"Yessir," Prince said. "Can't be nothing else."

"This man was a civilian employee from the fort," McMann said furiously. "Here to inspect beef tomorrow. Evidently you killed in self-defense, Buck, but you might use better judgment. Do you know what this means?"

"Well, hell," Buck said easily, "I reckon you'll have to find another beef inspector. I'll volunteer. I sure God know them cows pretty well."

A ripple of laughter traveled the edge of the room and choked off abruptly as McMann glared at the crowd. He began a speech, thought better of his words, and nodded to Adams. "Take care of it," he said, and marched straight-shouldered from the saloon.

In the following silence Adams said, "Prince, take this body to the icehouse, bring all the effects to my office. Gentlemen, return to your pleasures."

"That's all?" Buck asked.

"The verdict is self-defense," Adams said. "But let me

remind you that friends of the deceased are upstairs. I suggest you get out of town, Buck."

"How many friends?" Buck asked.

"Three."

"Tell them to get out of town," Buck said.

"Buck," Adams said sharply, "take a ride!"

Adams walked briskly from the saloon as the bartender tolled off half a dozen unwilling pallbearers and began the cleanup work. Before the back door slammed the games were underway, the bottles were tilted, the pool table was echoing to the cue ball's click. Glendon turned into the lobby beside Joe Jones and put his thoughts into words:

"That's how they do it here?"

"Legal and above board," Jones said. "Clear case of self-defense."

"No sheriff," Glendon said. "No marshal or coroner?"

"Adams is both."

"Both what?"

"Coroner and J. P.," Jones said. "No charges, no trouble. You heard him."

Glendon said, "Yes, I heard him," and walked from the lobby and stood deeply troubled in the porch shadows. He did not doubt that Buck had shot in self-defense, but the law in Fort Ellis was plainly a mockery. It was a shock to come from country where the law proceeded in an orderly manner no matter the circumstances and find no law whatsoever—for that condition was always the forerunner of justice being squeezed malleably between one man's hands; and one man was prone to use the law to advance his own interests and reduce justice to his personal whim. Glendon wanted to go home and forget tonight; instead, he stood rooted on the porch and waited for Buck.

McMann roamed the upstairs office, venting his spleen on the walls and the desk. They had finished a stormy session with the colonel's representative from the fort, packed that man and the two remaining drovers off to bed, and sat now in mutual anger.

"The fool!" McMann said for the tenth time. "The brainless young fool!"

"I agree," Adams said tonelessly, "but he was provoked."

"Who cares?" McMann said bitterly. "With fifty blockheads he could shoot, why does he pick a man from the fort?"

"I told you," Adams said.

"You told me what?"

"He's a killer," Adams said. "He's dangerous, and he'll be worse in a few weeks."

"Dangerous?" McMann snorted. "There was nothing dangerous about tonight. That damn fool from the fort was drunk. They just told us he was no good with a gun. What's dangerous about shooting such a fool?"

"That's the point," Adams said wearily. "Buck can't stop to gauge character, measure another man's gun speed. He simply doesn't care, Sam. He'll react the same way to any man. Now forget it. It was self-defense and the colonel must recognize that fact. I'll have it all cleared away in the morning."

"And I'll have the colonel on my neck at noon," McMann grumbled.

"Can't you handle him?"

"Of course I can handle him!" McMann said. "But he'll insist that we show some semblance of law in town. I can talk him out of that, I think, but tell Bailey I don't want to see Buck in this town until I give permission."

"Gladly," Adams said, "but I doubt it will matter."

"Why not?"

"If Buck decides to visit us," Adams said, "he will come a-calling. As for law, you have an experienced marshal honoring us with his presence."

"Shotgun Glendon!" McMann smiled mirthlessly. "I told you I had a feeling about him."

"Then see him," Adams said. "Sound him out. Perhaps he needs money. Maybe he'll take orders."

"You read the letter," McMann snapped. "He's one of those honest fools. Exactly the kind I don't want within fifty miles of here. And lost his guts, to boot. Oh, I'll talk to him, don't worry. I'll give him a week to clear out."

Manuel Martinez crouched behind the warehouse dock and spoke to the thick-set man beside him. Other men guarded the dock corners and, deeper to the east behind the corral, more men waited with the horses. John Colter listened silently while Manuel talked, showing remarkable calm in the face of bad news. He did not speak until Manuel finished, then he said, "Leslie see it?"

"No, senor. He was home."

"An' Buck was ordered out of town?"

"Yes, senor. They will go to Sherman. I heard them say so earlier."

"Let 'em go," Colter said.

"And here?" Manuel said. "What of your cattle, senor? Five hundred head. That is too much to swallow!"

"Just stretch your big mouth a little wider," Colter said. "It ain't time yet. I'll tell you when."

"Very well, senor."

"Now watch Leslie close," Colter said. "I think he's getting greedy and nervous both."

"He is that, senor."

"An' watch close if he makes a pass at McMann or Adams," Colter said. "He ain't jumped that way yet, but he might."

"Not yet," Manuel said. "He stays to himself."

"Unnatural," Colter said. "There's more to that hombre than he shows. Adios."

"Adios, senor."

Manuel watched John Colter walk away to the horses, mount, and ride eastward with his twenty picked men. Manuel remained a minute in the dock blackness, rolling a cigaret, staring thoughtfully into the night. Manuel Martinez was getting impatient with the progress of this affair. But like Colter, for whom he had worked five years, Manuel had remarkable patience. What rankled in his chest was playing janitor, mopping floors, unpacking boxes, taking orders from a cabron of Leslie's caliber. Manuel had swallowed about all he could stomach. Time was running out for Leslie and that ungodly pair across the street.

Charley Leslie was half-dressed when the shooting occurred. He slipped on his trousers and soft leather slippers, and circled through the back lots to the saloon, where he crouched at the rear window above the cellar door and watched the activity inside. He was forced to decamp when the bartender's crew headed for the icehouse with the body. Leslie moved off to the north, crossed the road, and came back along an adobe wall toward the rear of his store. Stopping at the wall corner he heard the soft voices and crouched before Colter's guard saw him. He could not distinguish individual words but he recognized Colter's rumble and Manuel's softer bass. Leslie waited until Colter and his crew were gone, and Manuel had strolled off toward the street; then he stood and shook himself like a wet dog.

"The old bastard!" Leslie whispered. "Hiding his right hand from his left!"

They were cooking up something behind his back, and the

only possible scheme was directed against McMann. But why do so without explaining such a plan to him? He could only infer that he was about to become the clay pigeon between two factions. He was only guessing, of course, but from tonight forward he dared not stand still and wait for the explosion. A smart man jumped first, and always feathered his nest in midair.

Charley Leslie circled wide to the south and came around into the livery barn through the back door, up the alleyway to the office where the night man slept on a cot beside the desk. The night man, Joe Jones, had drifted into town a month after Leslie's arrival and got the barn job without trouble. Jones growled at doing work far below his capacities, but he had teamed with Leslie too long to doubt the tall man's plans.

Jones woke quietly when Leslie whispered, "Joe," through the screen door.

"Charley?"

"Don't get up," Leslie said. "Listen."

"Fire away, Charley."

Leslie spoke rapidly for ten minutes. When he paused for breath, Jones sat up on the cot and rubbed his beard stubble. "Let me go over this," Jones said. "We're in the middle and we've got to get ready for a fast jump. We'll need a wagon and good team, have to load our stock at night and me clear town with it before daylight. Take it down the road, sell in any town between here and El Paso. Right?"

"Right," Leslie said. "Go on."

"Then come back and stay out of sight until you give the word."

"I don't know when this will break," Leslie said. "Meanwhile watch everything and everybody. I'll have more to go on in a few days. Good-night, Joe."

"Good-night, Charley."

Leslie left the barn as quietly as he came, padded back to his house, and undressed in darkness. He had promptly obeyed one cardinal rule of the game: protect your flanks by enriching your pockets as you took the fastest route out of trouble. But that move could take place only after Colter made a previous move and Leslie himself countered by testing McMann. And even then he took a chance if something was set to explode between the two. No matter, he thought, if they want a game he'd give them all a run for their money.

Glendon was turning off the porch for home when Buck and Ed Bailey appeared suddenly beside him, sweaty-smelling shadows in the night. He wondered how Buck felt and could not see the face clearly in the darkness; and then Buck touched his arm.

"We're leaving tonight, Pat. Come on along."

"Buck—!" Ed Bailey said urgently.

Buck swung around and placed one elbow in Bailey's ribs. He made no other gesture, and Bailey grunted acceptance of Buck's wish.

"Pat," Buck said. "Are you comin'?"

"Come down to the house," Glendon said. "Take a bath before you go."

"You got a tub, Pat?"

"I've got a bucket," he smiled. "Plenty of water."

"Get up behind me," Buck said happily. "Ed, let's slice these whiskers and get us a town bath."

Glendon mounted behind Buck and guided them through the back lots to his house. While they tied their horses Glendon lit his lamp, put the wash boiler on the fire, and toted water. When Buck entered, carrying his blanket roll, Glendon saw his face in the lamplight and paused a brief moment over the stove, coffeepot above the nearest lid.

Buck's face stood forth against the outer darkness like a chiaroscuro, white against black, lacking the weather-tempered colors of Ed's face, giving Glendon only a feeling of black and white, of starkness, with no intermediate shades. The lamplight was a bull's-eye, impaling Buck in center target; and the round face with the laughter and the soft smile that came so readily was not the same. Buck had stepped a little closer to an invisible boundary tonight; and Glendon could not ride along to Sherman and rub shoulders with that. Then Buck moved forward and took razor and soap from his bedroll, and the spell was broken.

"First come, first served," Glendon said. "I'll have coffee in a jiffy."

Ed Bailey trailed inside reluctantly and stepped against the wall and watched Buck pour a basin of warm water and start shaving in Glendon's mirror. When the boiler bubbled and Buck carried a bucketful outside to wash, Bailey came forward to shave. Shirt off, facing the mirror, Bailey kept his flickering glance on Glendon in the glass. Bailey was a suspicious man, years deeper in their game, a man who had learned his lessons the dangerous, dirty way and gave no lead rope to any man he did not totally understand.

"You coming along?" Bailey asked.

"No," he said.

Bailey scraped his jaw and flipped suds from his razor; a souse of soap, glancing off the blade, struck his cheek and made him wince.

"Glendon," he said. "Are you level with Buck?"

"All the way," Glendon said. "I've got no bone to pick. What's on your mind, Ed?"

"Buck," Bailey said softly. "He likes you."

"I like him," Glendon said simply. "Is that a crime?"

"Enough to throw in with us?"

"No," he said. "I'm not the style for your game, Ed."

"He wants to be your friend," Bailey said. "It can cause him trouble. How can you be amigos and stay outside?"

"I don't know," Glendon said, "but I won't preach to him. He can visit me any time, I'll cause him no harm. Folks have worked it out before, maybe we can do the same."

Ed Bailey said, "Maybe—" and shut his mouth as Buck came, jaybird naked, into the kitchen and began rubbing dry on his dirty shirt.

"Feels good," Buck grinned. "Go soak yourself, Ed."

Bailey dried his razor carefully, cased it, and carried a fresh bucket of hot water outside. Buck began dressing in clean underwear, then socks, a blue shirt, finally sitting on the stool to heel his boots and draw them on.

"Well," Buck said. "You coming?"

"No," he said. "Can you savvy why?"

"You taken a hand here in town, Pat?"

"None," he said, "and don't intend to."

"I savvy," Buck said. "You don't want to chouse cows or ride with us, an' that's all right. I never forced a man, for no man forces me. If you came along, we'd have some fun but no more. But it wouldn't be like just fun for you, eh?"

"Not very easy," Glendon said. "But any time you want to come here, you come. And I could do with riding out and seeing this country, Buck."

"I'll find time for that," Buck smiled.

Bailey appeared in the door, buttoning his shirt, slapping back his wet hair. Bailey said, "Thanks, Glendon. Sure appreciate it. Buck, time to go."

Buck stood to buckle on his holster, patted the Colt, and strapped his blanket roll. He paused at the door to say, "Pat, I had no choice tonight," and was gone across the yard. Glendon heard them walk the horses away toward the road where other men waited. Their hoof echo died in the night, one last defiant shout floated back, wild and free, and they were gone.

Glendon lifted the boiler off the stove and replaced the lids. He was pouring coffee when Swift Stamm knocked and entered. Glendon said, "Excuse the muss," and motioned to the coffeepot.

"I'll have a cup," Swift said. "I started over a while ago but you had company."

"Buck and Ed Bailey," he said. "Shaved, took a bath, just left for Sherman, wherever that is."

"Upriver," Swift said. "Pat, I heard a shot. What happened?"

He told her, pouring coffee and filling a plate with cookies she had baked two days ago. She sat at his table and spoke her blunt thoughts: "How do you know them?"

"Accident," he said. "I met Buck at Cross C."

He told her of the meeting, and some of his liking for Buck colored his voice, for her head lifted and he saw the puzzlement.

"I know Buck," she said, "and the rest of that crew. Do you know what Adams thinks of Buck?"

"I can guess," Glendon said. "Adams would call him a killer, probably wants to get rid of him."

"You're too close for comfort," Swift said. "Adams has told me how he feels. Pat how do *you* feel about Buck?"

She was trapping him, perhaps innocently, and if he talked his own past could not remain hidden; the lessons learned would show in his words. He said slowly, "I'm holding no case for Buck. He killed a man tonight and it affected him no more than rain water on a duck. He left here singing; he'll forget it tomorrow. That's wrong. Any way you look at it, that's dead wrong. You can't kill a man and let it slide off that easy unless—"

"Unless?" she said quickly.

"Buck's a funny boy," Glendon said. "I don't know where he came from, what's behind him, but he's riding the rail these days. One side of him is all laughs and fun, having a good time. He's generous, if he likes a man he makes a friend, and I think he values friendship because he hasn't had much of it. That's the good side. The other"— Glendon drank coffee and moved unwillingly into the skein of words that marked him, that told of dangers met and men known, of experience that had brought a dozen Bucks under his eyes—"is bad. Buck's riding a rail and he can tip either way in the time it takes to say the word. I've seen it happen before, I know how it comes to a boy like Buck.

"Look at him now, Swift. He's stealing cattle from Colter, selling them to McMann, and it means nothing to him but easy money. He'll spend it in a little while and come back for more. Never mind, I've seen men go that far wrong and still end up decent. But you kill a man—and I hear tonight was number four—and that works inside a boy the wrong way. Especially when it is so easy, when there's no law, and what law there is on his side. Then one day something tips the scales and he's gone, over the wrong side of the rail."

"And yet you like him?" she said.

"I like him now," Glendon said, "for the good part in him. Just as I'd like any man who treated me honestly, who offered me friendship with no strings."

"But if he changes," Swift said. "Goes off the wrong side of the rail, as you call it. What then?"

"That would end it," Glendon said bluntly. "Because there would be nothing good left in him. Take away the good part of a man, and it starts going when he starts killing, and you've got nothing left but a killer. I can never abide a killer."

"How can you say that?" she asked.

"You're drawing me out," Glendon said. "Yes, you are, and I think you know why. I've known too many killers, Swift. I've lived in Kansas and you've heard the stories out of Kansas the last few years. Stories about so-called gentlemen with a gun. Tear that tinsel away, all that romance those Eastern writers build up around a killer. It means less than the cheap words they write, the cheap stories they spread. There is no apology for a killer, he can give no valid excuse for his action. And once he starts, he never stops. Believe me, I know."

"You should," Swift Stamm said softly.

"Why do you say that?"

"I had to see you tonight," Swift said. "McMann received a letter from Kansas City this morning. I open his mail and arrange it for him. I don't need to tell you what that letter said, do I?"

"I kept hoping it wouldn't follow along," Glendon said. "Yes, I can guess what it told him, but tell me anyway."

"You've been a town marshal," Swift said. "A United States marshal, a county sheriff, a stagecoach guard. For the past ten years, in Nebraska and Wyoming and Kansas. Last in Kansas, and you resigned a month ago because, the letter stated, you lost your nerve. Is that true?"

"Yes," Glendon said. "I lost my nerve. You can't keep it up forever, Swift. Do you want to know how I felt those last months?"

"No," she said gently. "Because I don't believe it."

"What part of it?"

"Losing your nerve."

"You don't know," Glendon said. "You don't know me. What I was, how I lived, what I did for ten years. I lost my nerve, only they call it guts. Swift, I'm no gunman, no fast-draw expert. I carry a Colt but that's the last gun I used. I used a rifle some, but mostly a double-barrel ten-gauge shotgun with the barrels sawed off two inches past the forearm. You know what that gun can do? I know, because I used it. What did the letter call me? Shotgun Glendon?"

"Yes," she said. "That was the name."

"I earned that name," Glendon said flatly. "Staying alive, doing my job. Keeping the peace and carrying out the letter of the law. I've got no time for the Wild Bills and the Earps. Some of 'em wore a star at times, some never did, it made no difference. They're all killers, and they all live to start trouble and destroy peace. But I never saw the day they wanted to look that shotgun in the muzzle. I was a pretty good marshal, Swift. I believed in the law, in keeping the peace and giving every man a fair share of justice. I was paid for that and I like to think I gave full value. But doing it I made a lot of enemies, and finally it caught up with me. I was tired of wondering when I'd get it. I'm getting old, I'm going nowhere. I resigned last month and got out of town the same night. I damn near rode a good horse to death going as far south as I could before day. And I kept on riding, and I'm not done yet. All I want is to be left alone."

"Did you bring that shotgun?" Swift asked.

"I brought one Colt and one Winchester," Glendon said.

"Then I believe you," she said. "But I still say you haven't lost your nerve. I don't have to be a man to understand that. I lost my nerve two years ago, or thought I did. I suppose you've heard how by this time?"

"Yes," he said. "I heard about it."

"I lost my nerve," she said. "I was like a chicken with my head cut off for over a year. Then I woke up one day and knew it wasn't true, it didn't matter that I was alone. I'd

been alone before Bill was shot anyway, he'd gone away
from me and we couldn't get it back. I just didn't want to
admit that. So I did, finally, and now I'm all right. That's the
way it is with you, isn't it? You're looking for something and
some day you'll find it and then you'll be all right again."

"I hope that's it," Glendon said. "I couldn't say it was so
tonight. But we ought to rein off. Thank you for telling me
about that letter, but it won't do McMann any good. I can't
help him and he sure as hell can't help me. I'm not bothering
him. I want to stay here and fish and go to bed without
dousing my lamp first. That's all I want."

"If he lets you," she said.

"Swift," he said quietly, "don't get all worked up over me.
There's no reason."

"I like you," she said. "We can talk and you don't care
how I dress or what I do. You let me be what I want to be.
We can sit here and talk, and I can't do that with anybody
else."

"There's Leslie," he said. "He likes you a lot."

"And you've seen Leslie," Swift said curtly. "Why do I talk
to him? Because there was nobody else and at least he
doesn't—" she blushed and carried her cup to the dishpan
and stayed a minute before she turned. "Charley's cold inside. He has no real feelings. Pat, don't you want to talk with
me?"

"More than anything else," he said honestly. "But don't
start worrying about me. There's no future in it."

"All right," she said. "And I know you well enough to see
that you're getting worried about me. I should be home like
all respectable ladies. Good-night, Pat."

"I'll walk along," Glendon said.

He saw her halfway across the lot to her house and stood
in the darkness until her lamp moved in the north window;
and he thought of her in this godforsaken place, living this
way while outside in the other world people were doing all
the things she had surely dreamed of doing: the clothes and
the food and the fun of life that everyone should taste at
least once; and here she could only dream and hope while the
dream faded every day. But she did not complain; she went
on the same way and no one could read her thoughts. He
wondered what she was thinking, what she really wanted—to
get away, to stay, or what?

He returned to his dirty dishes and his coffee grounds and

the shreds of his own hope he had ridden so far to achieve. He looked around the house and packed his gear in his mind; ten minutes and he could be on the trail. Maybe he'd have to do it in less; but thanks to Swift he was forewarned.

Chapter Three

HOT, BURNING SUNLIGHT pursued them into the old town slumbering near the river beneath the ancient cottonwoods that shed bark rough as crocodile skin and fluff of nacreous luminosity. After the army abandoned it, the people had crept back to inhabit the barracks and officers' row, the stable and hospital and outbuildings; the hoof-hammered parade ground became the plaza and adobe houses grew facing that brown earth now reverting to grass. The streets meandered aimlessly, the roads curled into the blankness of the compass points; and no one rushed toward life in Sherman where tomorrow would be no better than yesterday. The gardens grew beside the acequias, hay and grain land flashed green along the river, cattle grazed on the nearby slopes. No child went hungry, but no man amassed wealth from the earth. The town was; therefore they lived. One visit gave a stranger the feel; if he returned he felt the leisurely tempo slow his blood.

Buck sang all the way across the plaza into the saloon that stored delightful odors of beer and whisky and homemade wine; and the owner, Coyote Smith, stroking his long mustaches, came forward in smiling greeting and set up the first round on the house. They drank at the tables beneath the time-darkened vigas in the coolness that felt richer than ice. Coyote Smith's wife served breakfast and smiled on them, for they had no enemies in Sherman. Ed Bailey was the first to walk slowly through the rear court toward the rooms and fall asleep on the rawhide-strung bed covered with a strawtick mattress and one patched blanket. The other three soon followed, leaving Buck alone at the table, squinting lazily at the sunglare framed in the door.

"What happened?" Coyote Smith said. "Last time there was ten of you."

"Oh, we left out with ten," Buck said. "Took our time and had us a poker game last night."

"An' five of you won?"

"Si," Buck laughed. "Other five had to sell some cows over in Texas. They'll be along directly. . . . Dance tonight?"

"Big fandango," Coyote Smith said. "Same as always."

"Get somebody to take the horses," Buck said.

He walked from the saloon and around the corner on the street leading to the river, and stopped under the tree he remembered so well. He had a clear view of the house from here, fifty yards back toward the plaza. He had walked the girl home and saw how the cottonwood towered over all others and cast a huge shadow against the night sky. She talked enough to explain that her husband was overdue from working across the river. She didn't encourage him, but she didn't tell him to stay away. Buck rolled a cigaret and watched the house; once the chimney smoke slacked off from breakfast fire, he saw the man leave for the plaza.

He was a young fellow, tall and thin, wearing cotton pants and a blue gingham shirt and runover boots. His teeth flashed white when he turned to smile a last goodbye, he wore his black hair slick and boasted one of those big-saddled noses. Buck watched him out of sight with a smile of good will; if the young fellow gave no trouble he'd be meek as a lamb himself. Buck walked slowly toward the house, ducked under the clothesline, and stepped into the kitchen. She whirled from the stove with a tiny shriek, recognized him, and smiled.

"Juanita," Buck said. "You remember?"

"Buck," Juanita Lopez said. "You are back."

"Just got in," Buck said. "You coming to the dance?"

"Oh yes," she said. "And you will be there?"

"With bells on," Buck laughed. "Do I get a dance?"

"Of course," she said. "You and your friends are always welcome here, Buck."

She spoke warmly but she kept the table between them, and she glanced through the front door with a toss of her long black hair. She concealed her nervousness with great effort; her husband was too close. Buck said, "Just wanted to say hello," and retreated through the doorway and saw the smile widen on her face. She was happy to see him, and happier to see him go. He walked to the river with her image in his mind, magnified by time. She was taller than most Mex girls, no more than eighteen, rounded and yet slim, moving in such a way that she seemed all curves and soft cavities. Buck liked her face, too; she had full, thick lips and high cheekbones and those big eyes, and her face was alive and sensitive without the coarseness so many of them showed. Buck turned under the cottonwood and saw her skirt flash in the kitchen shadow. He laughed and walked whistling up the street to the plaza.

Ed was snoring when he ducked into the adjoining room and undressed. Buck slept dreamlessly through the day and woke to shave, soap off, and dress in his clean outfit. He found Ed and the other boys in the saloon, talking with people they knew, buying drinks and laughing at jokes, waiting for dance time. Buck shook hands all around, bought a round, and played cooncan until Coyote Smith called, "Barracks are open," and untied his white apron.

They trooped around the plaza to the barracks that now served as town meeting place and dance hall. Lamps were hung from wall brackets and the orchestra was on a raised platform, violins and guitars and a goat-head drum. Everyone came to the dance, listened to the music, spread the latest gossip, watched the newest romance blossom. Coyote Smith closed the saloon, so liquid refreshments were carefully stored outside to bridge the arid spell. Buck danced with Smith's wife and kept looking at the benches as they spun; and finally he saw her, in a group of girls, her eyes laughing, her lips red, her feet tapping to the music.

"You know Juanita Lopez?" he asked.

"Oh yes," Lola Smith said. "Her husband works for us, with the sheep across the river. A good man."

"Where is he tonight?"

"He had to go back again," Lola said. "There was some trouble."

"Too bad," Buck said. "Somebody ought to dance with her."

"Well, go," Lola smiled. "I cannot compete with the tender ones her size."

"You're my girl," Buck said.

"Oh, go on!"

Buck crossed the floor and stood beside her, and the girls gave him those long-lashed glances of welcome. Buck smiled at them and faced her.

"Come on," he said. "You promised."

She danced away with him, not too close but moving not too far away. Buck was cautious while recalling all the steps he had learned in Chihuahua, until they were whirling with the music and she was smiling dreamily. When the set ended he took her to the corner, bowed to the other girls, and went away. He stepped outside and had a drink from Ed's bottle and rolled a cigaret. You could dance once but any more attention to one girl started the old tongues clacking like knitting needles.

"Laying your groundwork?" Bailey asked.

"Me?" Buck said innocently. "I ain't done a thing."

"I saw her," Bailey said. "Don't blame you, but she's married."

"He's nursing sheep tonight," Buck said. "She can't go walking home alone."

Bailey hunkered down against the barracks wall and cradled the bottle between his hands. He made a vague gesture toward the plaza and shook his head.

"They like us here. Time might come when we need one place to go. Don't spoil it, Buck."

"Won't spoil a thing," Buck said.

"Your funeral," Bailey said. "Not mine."

Buck wandered inside and danced a few sets with older women, and waited patiently until the orchestra bowed goodnight. He caught her in the darkness, took her arm, and guided her around the barracks. She said, "Please, it is not necessary," and felt his hand tighten. He walked beside her down the dusty street to the house, through the front door, where she turned and smiled.

"You are very kind," she said. "Thank you."

"How long does he nurse those sheep?" Buck asked.

"Oh, not long," she said. "He will be home soon."

"Nice house," Buck said.

She backed away, struck a chair, and hurried around the table. Buck followed and took in the room in one glance: hard-packed dirt floor, white-washed adobe walls, table and chairs and bed handmade from adze-cut lumber, two Navajo rugs and a Chimayo blanket—blues, grays, blacks and browns interwoven—and the stack of pinon wood beside the corner beehive fireplace.

"Buck," she said fearfully. "You must go now."

Buck closed the door and dropped the latch bar. He grinned as he crossed the room, watching her retreat from the table. He circled quickly and caught her beside the bed, still grinning, laying his big hands on her shoulders.

"My husband," she said. "He will—"

"Be out all night," Buck laughed. "I ought to know. I spent time with those damn sheep."

"No," she said. "Please—"

"You waste too much time," Buck said. "Nothin' ever come of talk."

One of the five missing poker players reached Sherman an hour before sunrise and pulled Ed Bailey upright in bed. Bailey yanked on his pants in the chill false dawn and heard the bad news: the five losers had cut a bunch of cows from Colter's main herd and driven on for the Texas line. They topped a ridge and met two Colter riders headon; one got away but the other man was killed. Four of the losers went on with the cows; the fifth had ridden a good horse half to death getting back to Sherman. Not because the death of one man meant more than a grumble to Colter; but the dead man was Colter's foreman. That quick flurry of shots had spelled the end of armed neutrality for them all.

"Roust 'em out," Bailey said.

He found Buck's room empty and ran for Juanita Lopez's house; and arrived just in time to see her husband enter, hear the shot, and run cursing toward the doorway. Buck appeared immediately, buttoning his shirt, backing outside with his Colt held carelessly on the darkness within. Bailey heard Juanita sobbing and caught, beneath that high-pitched sound, the groans of her husband. Then Buck holstered his Colt and spoke to the darkness.

"You ain't hurt bad. I shot you in the leg on purpose, but you ought to know better than come busting in that-away. Now you get a doctor, an' next time I come calling you stay with the sheep, hear?"

Then Buck turned and nudged Bailey toward the plaza. He finished buttoning his shirt as they walked, and finally laughed. "Damn idiot! Imagine him pulling such a fool trick. What you doin' up so early, Ed?"

"Getting you up," Bailey said. "We're leaving for Fort Ellis."

"But I'm not broke yet," Buck said reasonably.

"Nor likely to be," Bailey said. "McMann'll be looking for us."

"What happened?"

"Steve just got in," Bailey said. "Had trouble over east, shot a Colter man."

"Hell," Buck said. "John's got fifty men. He won't get riled up over losing one jughead."

"He will on this one," Bailey said. "The boys shot his foreman."

A tall man with an undershot jaw and heavy, sagging jowls walked laboriously into the Cross C yard, legs quivering from a twenty-mile hike. He entered the big house and brushed the protesting maid aside to get John Colter out of bed and tell his story of the five men who stole cattle and shot Cross C's segundo and gave his own horse a lungshot that drained its life twenty miles from home. His name was Pasqual, next man in rank to the dead foreman; and he shook with anger as he spoke.

"Patron," he said, "last week they took five hundred. Now more. And they shot Jack. Patron, this is too much."

"Easy, boy."

John Colter sat on the edge of his bed and rubbed his thick hands over his bare knees. Outside his window waking sounds touched his ears, dogs barked and roosters crowed, he smelled woodsmoke from the cookhouse and dew drying on the grass. Colter woke from a fine, dreamless sleep to lose his foreman, a man known and trusted for twelve years. A lesser man would climb the ridgepole and bay like a wolf; Colter's face betrayed no emotion.

"Five of them?"

"Yes."

"Then the other five went to Sherman," Colter said. "An' ain't spent all their money yet. That's good. Pasqual, you recognize any of the five?"

"Too much dust," Pasqual said bitterly. "Then we were shooting and I had to run."

"Don't matter," Colter said. "But you're right. I guess it's time."

"Say the word, patron!"

"Get those boys from the east camp," Colter said. "Now just you and me and Manuel know where they came from, what I planned. Keep it that way. Take 'em to Fort Ellis tonight and round up Manuel. Start it tomorrow morning right after breakfast. You remember how I want it?"

"I remember," Pasqual said.

"And Leslie," Colter said. "He won't know his ass from a hole in the ground about this. Wait till he shows up, stick a gun in his hands, make damn sure he does his share."

"He will," Pasqual said grimly.

"Boot 'em out," Colter said. "Burn the whole shebang."

"And McMann?"

"Kill the sonofabitch!"

Pasqual ran from the big house to saddle a horse and start his ride. John Colter climbed rheumatically into his faded overalls and patched shirt. He had planned this from the day he put Leslie into the store. Tomorrow morning seventeen men would start shooting across the street in Fort Ellis; they would keep shooting until McMann was dead or decamped. Either way, it was Colter's answer to three years of open theft, given in the only language McMann understood; and the beauty of it was, Leslie would take all the blame. For the fifteen men Pasqual was bringing in were all strangers, hired in Texas and kept at the east camp over a month. John Colter had paid them double wages to eat and sleep and wax fat; now they would earn their keep.

Glendon did not go uptown until the following Monday; at that time, heading for the store, Swift Stamm met him outside the livery barn.

"Turn around," she said.

She led him back to the barn corner, her fingers biting urgently into his arm. Even so, he saw nothing unusual in her appearance at this hour. She often did bookwork between six and seven, to escape the rising daytime heat. Glendon tried a smile to calm her down.

"What's the matter, you hook a trout already?"

"Trouble at Sherman," she said. "McMann and Adams were talking in their office. Buck shot another man up there Saturday night."

"Dead?"

"Buck was in a house with a girl," Swift said. "The husband came home, Buck shot him in the leg, they all came straight down here. They're in the cafe now."

"Why would they do that?" Glendon asked. "Shooting a man in the leg is no cause for such commotion."

"Let me get my breath," Swift said. "Pat, the reason they came back is a lot worse. I heard Bailey telling how they had a poker game on the way to Sherman. The five losers rode off to steal more Colter cattle and sell them in Texas. One of that bunch got back to Sherman yesterday morning. They met two Colter riders and killed one. He was Colter's foreman, a man named Jack Wilson. That's why Bailey brought them down so fast. You didn't know Wilson, Pat. He was the only man Colter really called his friend."

"Now the roof comes off?" Glendon said.

"There's more," Swift said. "Just a few minutes ago, after

Bailey talked, the major told Adams to offer you the marshal's job."

"Damned generous of him," Glendon said. "Yesterday he was ready to boot me out. Now he's hedging his bet."

"Pat, it makes no difference. You've got to leave right now."

"Wait," he said.

He held her arm and looked up the deserted street at the store fronts, the hitch rails, the tiny dust devils swirling before the boardwalk. He watched the silent town come alive. Manuel swept Leslie's porch and vanished into the store. Leslie appeared a moment later, taking his customary shortcut between buildings and across the street. The bartender slapped the saloon doors open, looked up at the sky, and turned inside; and one of Bailey's crew stepped from the cafe and picked his teeth on the porch. Glendon absorbed the stillness, the deceptive cool quality of early-morning peace, and the old fear rose in his chest. He would take no marshal's job but he detested the fear that whispered, "Get out!" For if he left he'd leave Swift in a dangerous town.

"Pat," she said, "Adams will come any minute."

His mouth shaped the words, "Very well," but his lips spoke other words that came from instinct. In that moment he saw Leslie's store windows smashed outward by rifle barrels, saw the entire store front erupt in flame, heard the roar of the shots, saw the man on the cafe porch tumble dead into the dust below the hitch rail. Glendon said, "Get back," and pushed her around the livery barn corner. He followed and pulled her along the barn wall and across the vacant lot to her house, where she sank on the nearest chair and stared at him numbly.

"Into the kitchen," Glendon said. "Stay away from the windows. Be back in two minutes."

He ran from her back door, hurdled the osage hedge, and raced for his own house. He scooped up his Colt and cartridge belt, the Winchester, six boxes of ammunition from the pantry shelf; and ran, hunched over, back to Swift's. She was in the kitchen, crouched against the wall below window line. Glendon ran through, latched the front door, swung the window shutters into place; then walked, catching his breath, to lean the Winchester against the wall and stand beside the small north kitchen window.

"What is it?" she said. "Why—?"

"We're lucky," Glendon said gently. "My God, we're lucky. If you had started five minutes later—but forget it.

That's Colter's answer, Swift, and we stay here until it's finished."

"But Charley's in his store," she said.

"We can't do a thing," Glendon said. "Listen . . ."

The rifle fire was steady, ricochets came off wood and iron to scream overhead, sailing across the river. The opening volley had been violent; now the sound was redoubled.

"All we can do is wait," Glendon said.

"But the innocent people," Swift said. "Mrs. Morales, all of them—"

"Dug in like us," Glendon said. "And just as safe. You had breakfast?"

"No."

"Well, I'm hungry," Glendon smiled. "You ought to be."

She rose from the wall and stood beside him, listening to the fight. She touched his arm and managed a smile.

"All right," she said. "Two over lightly?"

"And some of that apricot jam," Glendon said.

"Pat?"

"Yes," he said, watching the hotel.

"Nothing," she said quickly. "Thanks, just thanks."

He stared across the weedy lots at the gray-brown store backs; and knew how one moment in time could ruin a man's plans. He could not leave her until this business was finished; and listening to the battle with a professional ear, he doubted in all honesty that he could ever leave her. Once past youth a man's notions attained a depth of solidness; he found more in lesser things because he had passed the stage of inept longing. He could shoot a small deer, and the satisfaction was as great for him as a trophy head. Age endeared all lesser things in his eye; but when he looked for love, he wanted the absolute. He could not take a chance; he dared not guess wrong. And this was such a small hope, a beginning with no roots, certainly in the category of impossible dreams; but it had grown in him for three weeks. One-sided? It must be. He could offer her so little.

"Keep walking, senor!" Pasqual said.

Charley Leslie felt the gun and walked steadily down the center aisle into the warehouse; and saw many men waiting in the shadows. Manuel rose up and gave a signal; those men filed around Leslie and began crawling up the aisles toward the front window.

"Do you fight with us?" Manuel asked bluntly.

Charley Leslie understood everything, and silently cursed

himself for misjudging his time. He had never faltered in making quick decisions. He made one now, already exploring the future possibilities.

"Colter's orders?" he asked.

"Yes."

"Why didn't you let me know?"

"No time," Manuel said. "Do you fight?"

"Of course," Leslie said briskly. "Let's give McMann a bellyful."

He swung back into the store and went directly to the gun cases. He selected a rifle, began loading the magazine, and nodded toward the windows. "Going to kick them out?"

"Yes," Manuel said, from the floor.

"Then get these guns and the ammunition below window line," Leslie said. "Plenty of water in the warehouse?"

"Yes," Manuel said. "Before you came."

Leslie heard the reluctant note of approval in Manuel's voice. They understood authority, they respected a man who could keep his head. The tall one spoke to Manuel in staccato Spanish. Manuel smiled and crawled around beside Leslie.

"What does he want?" Leslie asked.

"He told me to help you," Manuel said. "So, you see, my janitor work is not finished. Let us get the guns down."

While they worked, Leslie watched the store front. The tall man was setting his line below the windows; and across the street one of Bailey's crew stepped outside and stood picking his teeth in the porch shade. The tall man cocked his Winchester and raised the barrel. Passing down the last case of ammunition, Charley Leslie watched the street, completely fascinated by the scene. The tall man whispered and fifteen rifles canted upward; he whispered again and fifteen men came off their knees.

"NOW!" the tall man cried.

The rifle barrels slashed forward, both windows burst into shards, the first volley was one deafening shot. Leslie saw the man on the porch roll lifelessly into the dust; then he was crawling across the store toward the beds and mattresses and bolt goods. He could only guess how this insane business might end; in the meantime he had no intention of stopping a bullet.

One moment Ed Bailey was sitting wearily at the cafe counter, coffee cup in his left hand; next a slug blew the cup into flying pieces and spun the handle around his forefinger. Another slug sliced the brim of Buck's hat and killed Steve in his tracks. The coffee urn toppled gracefully off the shelf and thudded on the duckboards behind the counter; coffee poured a tidal wave that scalded the waitress's feet. She screamed and ran for the kitchen; and Buck shot calmly past her head, emptying his Colt through the smashed window, placing his shots just above the sill line in Leslie's store front.

Bailey dove for the lobby arch and rolled through; the others hit the deck and crawled forward, fumbling for cartridges, skinning their elbows on the splintery floor. Bailey shouted up the hotel stairway; and McMann answered his call. Two men were dead in that first surprise volley; and the sun rose over Leslie's square false front and glinted off the dead man's belt buckle below the hitch rail. Buck walked into the cafe kitchen, dipped a cup of coffee from the cook's private sauce pan, and grinned at the waitress.

"Better take the back door," Buck said.

The cook threw off his apron and turned to follow, and Buck said, "Not you, amigo. You stay here. We'll damn sure be hungry before this is over."

The cook would repeat those words, with suitable embellishments, in the years to come; at the moment he could only drop to the floor and stare fearfully at Buck. Slugs were flying overhead, shattering dishware and puncturing pots, splintering the cafe walls; and Buck stood beside the stove, drinking coffee, grinning down at the cook.

McMann dropped his razor and ran, naked, to the stairhead. Ed Bailey shouted a hurried explanation and pointed across the street in emphasis. McMann lost no dignity in his nakedness as he listened to the rifle fire and barked his orders.

"Cover the front, put a few men in rear!"

McMann turned and ran the length of the hall, slamming his hand heels against the doors. By actual count he had twelve men upstairs—thirteen, with himself; downstairs a total of fourteen; and Adams was shaving in his rooms behind their offices. McMann gave a curt order to the first man dressed, looked down at his bulging stomach and unlovely figure, and returned to his rooms. He dressed quickly, already estimating the situation, planning his fight. For this was a battle to McMann; all the years of his life had trained him best for such moments. McMann strapped on a Colt, dropped the bulldog .38 into his hip pocket holster, and walked to the stairhead.

"Bailey!"

"Yo?"

"How many casualties?"

"Two," Bailey yelled, "but we're all set now, Major."

"You need more men down there?"

"Sure could use 'em, Major."

McMann faced the hall. "Five of you report downstairs to Bailey! You—the first five this way!"

They clattered past him, leaving a gap upstairs, and McMann realigned the remaining seven men in rooms facing the street; and hurried around the stairhead to the side hall door leading into Adams' rooms above the cafe. Adams was already shaved and armed, cheerful enough to offer a smile.

"Not entirely unexpected, eh?"

"Take over the warehouse," McMann said. "Move all weapons, ammunition, and blasting powder to a safe place. Issue all supplies. I'll be upstairs for the time being."

"Very well," Adams said, and then shook his head. "What in God's name is Colter's idea?"

"Simple enough," McMann said. "Pin us down, flank action tonight. Burn us out. I would employ the same tactics."

"And if he does?"

"He cannot," McMann said. "I intend to turn the tables on those ignorant fools. I will burn that store and kill every man in it. Don't expose yourself."

"Why, Sam!" Adams said. "Your solicitude is touching."

"Solicitude?" McMann said, from the doorway. "It's too damn much trouble finding another lawyer."

McMann weathered the surprise attack and launched an efficient rebuttal. Fire slacked off after the first hour's fighting, and the sniping began. McMann sent two men to the hotel roof; Pasqual countered with a man on Leslie's roof behind the false front. Toward noon McMann dispatched three men in a wide circle to kill or capture the horses in Leslie's corral. Pasqual himself greeted those men; two died and the third staggered back to the hotel with a torn arm. McMann sent a crew to rip the heavy timbers from his icehouse and build solid barricades behind his windows. In Leslie's, Manuel used every box, crate, mattress and cloth bolt for a similar purpose. McMann tolled off two relays of men, one firing, the other resting or performing tasks in rear. Pasqual kept five men up front, two guarding the store corral, two under the warehouse dock watching the flanks.

Through the town, no one moved; houses were dark and silent, dogs had disappeared beneath porches, chimneys were dead. No man, or woman, had tried to saddle a horse and ride for the fort; the town crouched behind adobe walls and waited on the final verdict. By mid-afternoon that verdict seemed a week away; they were fighting a stalemate under the blazing sun.

Buck had lain on his belly in the cafe and exchanged shots with the roof sniper until his nose itched from gunpowder and his face turned beet red. His only consolation was knowing that the sniper was clinging to a slanting roof, shingles hot under his boots, sun above making him dizzy, wanting water and unable to take the time as he moved up and down the roof behind the false front. But the boards were either too thick for a Colt, or the sniper was lucky.

"The hell with this," Buck said.

He went back to the store warehouse, selected a Sharps buffalo gun, and walked out and around the corner of the store. When Pasqual's sniper rose and snapped a shot into the cafe, Buck steadied the buffalo gun against the corner and sent a fifty-caliber slug through the false front, one foot below the cornice. The rifle came sliding off the roof; the man followed, cartwheeling to the ground. Buck blew smoke from the Sharps' barrel and returned to the hotel. As he walked up the back hall the man guarding the left front window raised his head to fire and took a shot in the face. Across the street Manuel levered another cartridge into his Winchester and grinned wickedly. Buck could not see Manuel but he stared at the dead man on the lobby floor and cursed softly. It was tit-for-tat; they were getting nowhere. Buck caught Ed Bailey's eye and motioned him back to the safety of the stairs.

"How many does that make?" Buck asked.

"Five," Bailey said. "An' a couple shot up."

"No good," Buck said. "They mean business over there."

"Maybe they're gettin' better pay," Bailey said dourly. "The major ain't said a word about that. I'd get out now if I could."

"Tonight," Buck said. "You an' me."

"Should I hit the major up again?" Bailey asked. "Might be worthwhile."

"Oh sure," Buck smiled. "If he's alive tonight to pay off."

Glendon managed an hour's sleep toward suppertime, and woke to souse his face in the wash basin and find a smile for Swift.

"What will they do?" she asked.

"Fight," he said. "Till somebody wins."

"How long is that, Pat?"

"I think it will end tonight," Glendon said.

"And who—?"

"Who wins?" he asked. "McMann has more men, but that other bunch is here to stay. I'm inclined to bet on them."

"But McMann will get help," Swift said. "From the colonel."

"No help there," Glendon said. "This is off limits for the army. McMann set up his town and made his own law. Now he's tasting the same medicine. Only way the army can step in is on orders from your territorial governor ... and who will let him know in time? Nobody."

"It's a terrible thing," she said. "I just can't believe this is happening, Pat."

Glendon said, "Still it happens. Now, when it gets dark, we want no lights. I'll be outside."

"Why?"

"Safest way," he said. "Anybody comes barging around, I can stop them before they get too close. I could do with supper if you're up to it."

"I'm up to it," she said, "but don't ask me how I'll feel in the morning."

McMann watched darkness cross the sky and smother the street below; rifle fire sputtered into silence as men went in relays to the cafe kitchen. McMann paced the upper hall, gnawing his thumb, planning for the night. He still had twenty-one able-bodied fighting men, while enemy casualties had cut their strength to a rough dozen. McMann planned a diversion for midnight, a direct-fire fight across the street, during which time he would send two flanking parties out to move upon Leslie's store. Then a calculated period of silence —say two hours—to lull all suspicions; and then an assault. That should come at approximately three A.M. when a man's spirit dipped to lowest ebb.

Those flanking parties would need coal oil, rags, and blasting powder bombs. They would carry shotguns and Colts for the infighting. It was now nine o'clock, giving him three hours to issue orders, prepare special equipment, reevaluate his plans for possible error. Well satisfied, McMann stepped away from the nearest door and lit a cigar. At that moment the entire set of buildings quivered to the smashing thud of a heavy object; someone had rammed a wagon into the north

saloon wall. Flame flickers danced redly in the hall window.
Rifle fire boomed from across the street.

McMann heard the surprised shouts as he ran to the
stairhead; even as he roared orders, men rushed toward the
danger. McMann charged downstairs into the saloon and
took personal command of the situation. He organized a
bucket brigade, sent the bartender with two men to hang
blankets across the saloon front to mask their movements.
Bailey led six men outside and around the corner; other men
passed sloshing buckets from the water barrels in the back
room. Within five minutes Bailey returned with his report.

"Cart," Bailey said. "We put it out."

"Now, by God!" McMann said. "We shall give them a
taste of stronger medicine."

The bar seemed to swell suddenly and slap him in the
chest. He was blown forward against the knurled edge, he
staggered backward and reached out blindly for support. He
fell over a card table as the concussion first deadened, then
seeped from his swollen eardrums; and he heard timbers
crashing, floors grinding apart, smelled acrid smoke on the
blast wind. In that moment McMann refused to admit his
mistake, recognize his own weakness; that he, as a military
man, should have known the hay wagon was a feint, that in
his own stubbornness he refused to credit ignorant fools with
such wit. They had tricked him with the hay wagon; and now
he faced a truth he could not believe, much less combat. His
world was coming apart before his eyes; his mind clouded
over and he walked unsteadily toward the hotel lobby, thinking only of escape.

Standing at the house corner, Glendon saw the blast ex-
pand redly, felt the explosion shake the town. The general
store and cafe roofs rose, collapsed, dropped upon their own
foundations. Men screamed and fire licked catlike at the
sudden ruins. Swift cried out inside and Glendon called,
"Come here," and led her away from the house to the
cottonwoods. They were safer here if panic started; fright-
ened men, racing from danger, stumbling against houses,
were apt to shoot blindly as they ran. Here she could lie flat
and minimize her danger.

"Lie down," Glendon said.

They stretched out beneath the trees and Glendon watched
the fire gain strength, surge high against the sky. He saw the
fleeting silhouettes of half a dozen men leave the livery-barn
shadow and spread across the vacant lots. Colter's outfit was

moving into position flanking McMann's rear. With gunfire from Leslie's store pinning down the street, McMann dared not stay inside. He had to run or roast. And when he brought his men through that back hotel door, it would be a wild and terrible moment. Glendon lifted his arm and laid it over her shoulders; and thought of the men inside, feeling their fear, speaking their words.

"They'll burn," Swift said. "Or run and——"

"Pray for them," Glendon said. "I can't do that, Swift. I know them too well."

For he did. In those rare moments of inner understanding the spirit probed deeply into all questions and lit up a lucky few like lamps shining in the night. He saw too much, disconnected perhaps, but full of meaning tonight: the sough of cottonwoods in the wind, his memory of the bartender in repose one afternoon last week, puzzled face above the brown-freckled arms and sop rag, asking without words whatever his thoughts might be; actors all in the play, some good, some bad, some like the trees, there because God willed it so.

Pasqual had pushed the hay wagon against the saloon and started the fire. He retreated immediately with his party to the crumbling adobe wall that ran parallel to the lots behind the hotel. When Bailey's bucket brigade rushed outside, Pasqual held his fire, let them douse the burning hay unharmed. For Manuel was running from the livery barn, around the store, to the junction of cafe and store walls where he wedged his heavy sack beneath the floor timbers and lit the fuse. Manuel ran to rejoin his party behind the livery barn, counting off the seconds in his head.

"Down," he said. "Cradle your chins, hombres. Open your mouths. She will go in a——!"

Manuel's head bounced against his cupped hands. The earth shuddered, they felt the blast and the wind rush, heard flying objects lift high into the night and arc downward with the sound of steel guitar strings. Manuel said, "Now," and led them to their prearranged line facing the back lots. Fire started in the shambles that was once cafe and store, shot upward, inched greedily into the hotel lobby.

"Be ready," Manuel called. "Any minute now!"

Buck was sleeping in the last hotel room on the back hall when the fire started. He sat up, rubbed his face, and listened. A few minutes later the blast spun him off the bed against the bureau. He rose unharmed as the cafe and store collapsed, then burst into flame. Leaping to the south window, Buck saw men run from the livery barn and take up a firing line facing the back lot. Buck tossed his Winchester aside, kicked off his boots, and dug his socked toes into the rag rug. A man had to travel light, the way they were headed. He stepped into the hall and waited beside the back door; and Bailey came running from the lobby with a dozen survivors. Fire was licking into the lobby, illuminating the hall, painting a greasy red patina on their faces. McMann shouted orders that made no sense; no one listened as they crowded around Buck. Bailey rapped his knuckles on the door and shook his head.

"Narrow chute," Buck said. "You got to try it, Ed."

"Jesus," Bailey said softly. "And them waitin' for us out there."

McMann shouldered between them and spoke gibberish that ended as Buck clouted him on the ear and spun him against the wall.

"Shut up," Buck said genially. "All right, boys. Run like hell and head for the river."

Bailey dropped his rifle and toed off his boots. The others followed his lead and stood waiting in dirty socks, in the smell of sweat, anticipating the harsh earth beneath tender soles—the stones and weeds, thorns and cactus, the rusty tin cans. One man spoke in refusal, giving more worry to his feet than value to his life. Bailey said, "Hell, wear your boots and die," and faced the door.

Buck yanked the door open and the night rushed upon them. Red light cross-hatched the back lot, flooding down from the gutted roofs, the corners, driving darkness far back beyond the icehouse, toward the river where the last orange streamers were swallowed by the night. The yard was a deathtrap; the rifles were waiting. Bailey hesitated, drawing his Colt, and heat from the lobby burned their necks.

"See you at the pens," Bailey said. "If I make it."

"You," Buck said, prodding the two men behind Bailey. "Lift your hocks. Fry or run."

Bailey broke from the doorway, the others close behind, and the rifles exploded from north and south. Bailey shot back and leaped high, bent down, slowed, speeded up, twisted toward the icehouse and yawed away. The second man dropped but Bailey was still going, very near the outer darkness when Buck lost sight of him and turned to throw the next man through the door.

"Run!" Buck shouted. "Rise and shine!"

His victim was the cook; and the man leaped into the night, apron-white, a perfect bull's-eye, bare feet slapping the earth. A white apron and a whiter face, stumbling and dodging, gaining the icehouse, going on with the luck of the blind; then the others were leaving the doorway and the rifles were firing as rapidly as hands could work the levers and follow moving targets in the flame-lit night. Adams stepped beside Buck, dirt-gouged wrinkles aging his face.

Adams would never again speak contemptuously of Mexicans. He had learned a single, lasting fact during the day and night: when all else failed such men they went straight to the only lasting solution—life or death. Adams ran, a pathetic figure, another man followed him and fell dead in two strides; and the rifles sputtered momentarily, reloading, and Adams tottered past the icehouse into dark safety.

"Well," Buck said. "Are you going or staying, McMann?"

McMann clung to the door frame, heat from the hall blistering his shirt. He yelled something and burst outward on his heavy legs, head thrown back, running without sight or thought. Buck watched him pass the halfway mark; then three-quarters as he reached the icehouse. As he stretched desperately for darkness a dozen shots kicked dust around him, smashed him down, rolled him over dead. Buck stood alone in the hall, pursing his lips in disgust. There went a meal ticket; but the way things had gone, they might as well strike out on their own.

Buck closed the door and turned into the bedroom, dumped the water pitcher over a blanket and draped it on his raised forearms; it provided a steaming shield as he ran up the hall into the lobby and fought his way through rising flames to the saloon. He stopped in comparative safety to catch his breath; and glanced back through the lobby at the cafe ruins. He saw the bullet-smashed shelves, the twisted walls, the tomato cans bleeding on the sugar spilled below. Buck ran to the back storeroom, picked his way between whisky barrels and beer kegs, and found the small side window boarded up long ago to prevent petty theft. He wrenched the boards away and boosted himself through the opening, fell head first to the ground, and rolled to his knees, Colt ready, still in darkness here as he had expected. He began crawling north, away from the fire and the town, into the night.

Charley Leslie was one of four men detailed to create the

pin-down fire from the store front during those final minutes. When it was finished and Pasqual led his men across the street, Leslie turned from the barricade and lit a cigar. He had learned a great lesson tonight: that you did not fight John Colter with a gun. Leslie stood beside his gutted showcase as they moved past him, carrying their dead and wounded, and he realized belatedly that no one in town had seen their faces, no one could name them.

"Well, Manuel," he said. "Are you going?"

"No, senor."

"Wise move," Leslie said. "They took over the store, we couldn't stop them, eh?"

"I am thinking that way," Manuel smiled.

"Then let's save this store," Leslie said. "Colter would appreciate that."

"You are right," Manuel said. "I will find a few brave souls."

"Tell me something," Leslie said. "Was this the only way to settle it?"

"Look, man," Manuel said softly. "The time comes when the only way that holds truth is death."

Yes, Leslie thought as Manuel disappeared, and he still had a stock of goods worth money down the road . . . if he wanted to go. Last night his plan was made; now he saw fresh possibilities in the future.

Glendon lifted her and led the way to the house. She faltered and he held her firmly while she cried at last, a necessary relief she had bottled up too long. Manuel hailed them a minute later from the front yard, asking for help.

"Right with you," Glendon answered.

"Charley," Swift said. "Is he all right?"

"Manuel?" he called.

"Si?"

"Leslie?"

"Unharmed, senor. Please come quickly and bring a bucket if you can. We will need much help."

Manuel charged off to the south, shouting into the other houses as he ran, and Glendon found the water bucket in the darkness and made her walk to the front door and step outside beside him.

"Now you go and see Mrs. Morales," he said. "We'll need coffee before the night's over."

"Pat," she said, "how did it end? What will happen now?"

"Tomorrow," Glendon said. "Don't give it a thought tonight. We'll know tomorrow."

Chapter Four

GLENDON SLOUCHED EXHAUSTED on a nail keg outside the livery barn, thinking dully how all of life seemed to be a process of getting hurt, licking wounds, and getting hurt again. He saw the people of the town crowded into the street before Leslie's store, staring apathetically at the smoking ruins of McMann's tiny empire. Only the half-melted adobe walls, jagged and black, marked what had been the greatest influence in their restricted lives. Those people had fought all night to save the balance of the town, fought with buckets and spades and soaked blankets they could ill afford to lose; now the damp, coarse odor of doused fire abused their nostrils, clung to their soot-stained bodies. They had saved the town; they had carried the dead to a common gathering place in the livery barn; and there, shrouded in a singed blanket, McMann slept unprotesting among lesser mortals. Those people had saved the town and lost three of their own to wild shots: an old woman, a man of forty, and a child of ten. Their deaths, unknown to Glendon until an hour ago when the bodies were collected, filled him with sadness and rage. McMann was gone but Glendon waited for the appearance of the man who lived. Adams was not a coward; he would not run away.

"Here comes Adams," Jones said. "By God, if he ain't a sight!"

Glendon swung around on the nail keg and saw Adams limping up from the river, a ragged scarecrow resurrected from the dead. Adams joined the crowd and established his old authority with a few eloquent gestures, a few sad words, proving the shrewdness of those men who turned weaknesses into virtues. Adams was alive and returned to the town, therefore he was a better, more virtuous man than McMann, who was dead. Now was the time to throw Adams out of town, give him no second chance to smother them with trouble. Instead, two men tenderly helped him up the steps into Leslie's store.

"The little bastard," Jones said. "They ought to cut him into tripes. He's laughing at 'em, you know that?"

"I know it," Glendon said tonelessly. "I know it too well, Joe."

He knew too well that life was basically a comedy, with a touch of comic in every tragedy. The man who could laugh at himself was rarely beaten; and the man who could laugh at the stupidity of others was heartless. Adams was certainly chuckling at his own macabre situation; but he was roaring inwardly at the fools who gave him another chance. He spent ten minutes in Leslie's store before he limped down the street toward Glendon. He had a gleam in his red-rimmed eyes, the look of a sinner turned righteous; no man became so righteous as a reformed sinner, and a false one at that.

"Joe," Adams said. "Is Sam inside?"

"Sure," Jones said gruffly. "An' all the rest."

"God rest their souls," Adams said piously. "I will handle all arrangements, pay all expenses. The padre will hold services this afternoon. Do we have caskets?"

"No," Jones said. "McMann never stocked them."

"Then do your best," Adams said. He plumped down on the ground beside Glendon and rubbed his dirty hands across his eyes. "Pat, I want to see you later on today."

"What for?" Glendon said. "I can't say the prayers."

"Don't be blasphemous," Adams said.

"I don't care about them," Glendon said bluntly. "Just three of them in there, Adams. I care about those three. Do you? Get on with it!"

"I won't argue with you, Pat," Adams said. "I've been through too much. I just sent a message to the fort. I begged the colonel to telegraph the governor. Last night was murder. We must have law and order in this county."

"You've changed," Glendon said curtly.

"Wouldn't you?"

"So now you want a sheriff?"

"I do," Adams said.

"Appointed by the governor?" Glendon asked. "Taking orders from the governor. You want that?"

"I do," Adams repeated. "His orders would be identical with my own wishes."

"I don't blame you," Glendon said. He rose from the nail keg and moved off, then paused to voice Adams' unspoken fears. "You better find some law fast. Ed Bailey and Buck won't be polite and wait on you."

"Pat—!"

He walked away before his anger got out of hand. Adams had played both ends against the middle so long that, like McMann, he had deemed his position impregnable. Now Adams knew all too well that Buck and Ed Bailey would run wild, feed off all factions impartially, laugh at all law. Adams was afraid for his life; and Adams wanted him to shoulder the burden.

"The hell with them all," Glendon said aloud.

He entered his house, heated water, and scrubbed his filthy body until the skin was red. He dressed in clean clothing, buried the dirty outfit in the garden, and walked on to the river. Sitting half asleep, he saw nymphs floating in a backwater eddy behind the old cottonwood log, insect larvae begging him to try an artificial fly. The bugs were most plentiful in cold, sweet streams with clean bottoms. You looked for larva cases on rocks at the waterline, searched for caddis and stick worms among underwater heaps of leaves and sticks. More nymphs might be clinging to the undersides of rocks, living in little houses pasted to the stones. His mind deliberately left the town and lingered over those pleasant, peaceful thoughts; but he was only fooling himself, dodging the truth. He would not forget last night and the three innocents lying among the guilty.

"I knew you were here," Swift said. "Come up and eat."

She had washed and changed into the well-worn clean trousers and blue shirt Glendon forever associated with the clean face and the clean mind. She carried sandwiches, coffee, and two cups hooked over one finger. Glendon turned from the water and joined her on the flat rock and ate with sudden hunger. The coffeepot drained, he rolled a cigaret and held it steady while Swift scratched a match across her trouser seat and lit the twisted, turned-up end.

"I saw Adams," she said. "He told me you had a talk."

"He talked," Glendon said. "I walked away."

"The news is already around town," Swift said. "Everybody hopes you'll take the job."

"Don't push it at me," he said roughly.

"I'm sorry, Pat."

"No," he said; "I'm sorry. Listen, there's not much left here. What will you do?"

"Adams wants me to stay," she said. "He's going to rebuild."

"With what?"

"Money," she said simply. "A lot of money. I copied the joint will they drew up last year; each gave the other everything in case of death. Adams has it all now."

"The meek shall inherit the earth," Glendon said thinly. "In a— Don't you want to get out of here, Swift?"

"I don't know," she said. "Every time I think so, I wonder where I'd go, what I'd do. Maybe I've been here too long to ever leave. Pat, I like these people. I don't want to see them hurt again."

"They'll be hurt again," Glendon said. "Say all the prayers and call all the law, they'll still get hurt again. Hell, you can see it in their faces. They've been born and bred to it for three hundred years."

"Maybe that's why I want to stay," Swift said. "Pat, will you take the job?"

"Nobody's made me an offer," Glendon said.

"Pat," she said. "I think you will."

"You mean, you want me to?"

"Yes," she said, and then, "No—I don't know what I mean."

"I know what you're going to do," Glendon said. "Go home and go to bed."

"And you?"

"Snoring in five minutes," Glendon smiled. "Come on, Swift. I'm not so young any more."

He pulled her to her feet and walked beside her from the river; when she reached the path fork and turned off she said, "No one is young any more, Pat. Maybe that's our saving grace.'"

He watched her go away, tall and slim, and wondered how much he ought to read in her words, how far he should look behind the new-spun fabric of their friendship. She had sensed his outrage today, his compulsion to do something for these people. She was sickened by last night but he saw it with different eyes, with wiser eyes, as a repetition of similar nights in distant towns. They saw death through different eyes, but their feelings were the same. She was innocently becoming his conscience, he thought, and all he could do was ride on or wait for a message from the governor. He was under no edict to stay; but he would, at least for a little while. And once the governor verified his record, he knew what the message would ask.

That afternoon Adams stood with the people of the town in the sunbaked cemetery ground. He shed a dry tear for McMann and returned to his temporary desk in Leslie's store. The king was dead—long live the king! Adams lit a cigar and took pen in hand. He wrote a dolorous letter to McMann's only known relative—that spinster cousin in Ohio—and told of Sam's untimely death by fire which destroyed the entire business. He had assumed all burdens—which meant expenses to that tight-fisted old gal—and he was hoping to salvage a few dollars from the ruins. No insurance, he wrote; he could offer no more than his condolences in this saddest of hours. Adams signed his name with a flourish. That took care of the relative.

He swung around and bent over the fire-blackened safe recently dug from the wreckage and carried here. He spun the dial, opened the heavy door, and placed the strongbox on his knees. The cash was unharmed, twenty-eight thousand dollars, and all his. He replaced the box, closed the door, and spun off the combination. When Charley Leslie came from the warehouse Adams called, "Sit down, Charley," and offered a cigar.

"Sad business," Leslie said. "I thought the padre did a fine job."

"Considering the antecedents of the deceased," Adams said. "Charley, let's talk."

"Fire away."

"I was Sam's partner," Adams said. "And his sole heir. I am staying here, I intend to start rebuilding tomorrow. But no business at the old stand. You savvy?"

"Yes," Leslie said. "That's smart."

"Once burned," Adams agreed darkly. "Times are changing, smart men make more money in other ways. Charley, I won't rebuild our store. I'll build a new hotel with attached bar and cafe, my offices upstairs. I want to sell the livery barn. Are you in the market?"

"God, no," Leslie said. "This is enough place for one man."

"Then power to you," Adams said. "Now, Charley—I'll mention no names, but the man who ordered this massacre is in for trouble. Ed Bailey and Buck are very much alive. They'll go after him tooth and toenail. He'll be so busy worrying about them that he might pull in his horns a bit. Does that give you any ideas?"

"Two," Leslie said. "First we are due for a dose of law.

Second, there could be a chance for somebody else to start ranching around here."

"Exactly," Adams said. "The law will take care of itself. I have recommended Glendon to the governor. How much do you know about him?"

"Nothing."

"Then bend an ear."

He told about Pat Glendon and was pleased to see mild surprise twist Leslie's face. He said, "If Shotgun Glendon takes the job, we'll have law and order. But he'll need deputies. I know you are asking the big question: can we control Glendon? The answer is no. But, let me repeat, he will need deputies. I think we should discuss that more fully if Glendon takes the job."

"Sure," Leslie said. "What about this ranch deal?"

"Just this," Adams said. "How much cash can you spare?"

"None," Leslie said, and grinned. "Don't get riled up. You've got a pokefull. You're giving me the store business free of competition and you're dangling rich bait under my nose. That's fine but I don't rush into anything. Let me think it over a week or so. Then we'll talk, cards on the table."

"One week," Adams smiled. "Cards up."

Charley Leslie went away to put his store in order. Working in front, whistling soundlessly as he stacked bolt goods and mattresses, he grinned to himself. Adams was plunging back into the old game as fast as he could rebuild; and last night had certainly changed the shape of things for Charley Leslie, esquire. Now he could afford to sit back and pick the ripest peach. He'd give Adams no definite answer until he heard from John Colter; and sure as the sun rose, he would hear from Colter.

Only three of them rode north from McMann's pens across the river. The others elected to cut and run for El Paso. Ed Bailey and Tom McMillan waited half an hour, holding Buck's horse, before they started up the trail; in that minute Buck came from the river, sopping wet, and mounted the black horse. They rode all night and made dry camp in the willows, slept through daylight, and rode on toward Sherman. Ten miles below town Buck sent McMillan forward to sound out the town's temper toward them. McMillan returned with two of the four men who had sold Colter's cattle in Texas. McMillan was all for going into town; the news hadn't come up the river and nobody was too mad at Buck for shooting Juanita Lopez's husband in the leg. Besides, he was damn near recovered.

"Let's go in," Ed Bailey said.

"We're riding east," Buck said flatly.

Bailey remained crouched beside the fire, scratching cabalistic dirt marks with a stick. He had expected this scene for two weeks, and now he took his time weighing chances. If he rode east, he gave up his leadership to Buck. If he refused Buck might start shooting. Bailey glanced beneath his hat brim toward Buck's boots, planted firmly across the fire. He had no reason to hate Buck. They had ridden too far together, shared too many experiences. Bailey was an honest man with himself. He knew his own shortcomings; and he accepted the truth. Buck was changing day by day; had changed more than anyone realized in the last few nights. Bailey threw his stick into the fire and looked up with a grin.

"All right, Buck," he said. "When do we start?"

Buck grinned and turned to his horse; but his smile lacked the good-natured laziness of yesterday. Buck led them from the trees to the river, and did not bother looking back. They followed, Ed Bailey riding rear guard. All through that day no words were spoken but they understood: Buck was the leader, Ed Bailey was second-in-command. They came at darkness to Colter's south camp, a line cabin and horse corral beside the windmill; and Tom McMillan's horse went lame.

Colter's camp man stood beside the tank and watched them water the horses. Buck shook out his rope and cut a fresh horse from the corral, pulled it protestingly through the gate. The camp man was only a thin-faced, gangly boy but he ran out to grab Buck's rope and give it a hard yank. Tom McMillan called, "Hell, boy. We're trading you my horse." But the boy started down the rope toward the Colter horse, and Buck said calmly, "We're wasting time." Buck shot once and the boy lifted his arms and fell away from the rope. Buck pulled the horse over beside the tank, tossed the rope to McMillan, and punched the spent cartridge from his Colt.

"Shift your gear," Buck said. "We've got cows to gather."

"God damn!" McMillan said softly.

"What?"

"Nothin'," Tom McMillan said. "Be switched in a minute."

Bailey cupped his hand against the windmill pipe and deflected the water against his face. He drank deeply and led his horse off a way and mounted. Buck had shot the kid in the back, and the kid wore no gun. Bailey had ridden through his own life and reached that moment when a man either turned back or crossed an invisible line and went on; and once he crossed there was no return. Then a man lived on until his string ended. He had watched Buck the past three weeks, wondered how near Buck was, when it might happen. The fight at McMann's was enough to change any man; but even then Bailey was not sure.

Now he looked at the body beside the corral gate and followed Buck eastward into the twilight. The moment had come and passed, so quickly Buck himself would be unable to name it later on, to say that was the time. But Ed Bailey knew, and rode on. There was no turning back for them now. They rode one road and it would squeeze narrower every passing day.

News gathered slowly in a country so vast. John Colter had his pipe line to the state capitol, but it took a week to bring him information that spread a wintry grin on his round face. So Adams was going back to business at the old stand, was he? So Adams had used his influence to request law and order in the county; and recommended Pat Glendon for the sheriff's job. Colter blinked calmly when his man from the capitol reviewed Glendon's past; but he grinned at the latest news, something Adams had evidently not heard. A change of governors was taking place, the new governor was arriving tomorrow from the east and it would take time before the new man—a general of the army—was ready to operate. Colter gave his man orders and sent him back to the capitol. Adams had influence, but John Colter was infinitely more powerful.

His man carried instructions to Colter's lawyers; that he, Colter, wanted law and order more than anybody else, that Glendon was a sound choice for the job—if the former Kansas marshal would accept. However, Glendon needed deputies and Colter recommended a man from Fort Ellis who also wanted peace and was such a good citizen he would accept a deputy's badge to the detriment of his own business. John Colter would be happy to meet the new governor and offer the benefits of his hard-earned knowledge if it would help, in any way, to mitigate the present situation.

Then John Colter gave succinct orders to Pasqual: ride to Fort Ellis and tell Charley Leslie to expect someone from the governor's office and answer yes to that man's question. There would be another deputy, of course, and that man should be of Spanish blood. Leslie was to recommend Manuel.

"At once," Pasqual said. "But what about Buck?"

The boy from the south camp had been found, the story read accurately in the tracks around the tank and corral; and two hundred head of prime stock was missing from the south herd. Pasqual and all the crew were on the bitter edge these days. They had liked the boy who worked so hard, listened eagerly to their advice, a boy found shot in the back, a boy unarmed but for the rifle left in the line cabin.

"Hold tight," Colter said. "Now I don't mean if you run into Buck. Just bring me his ears then. But we won't go lallygagging after him just yet."

"Yes, patron," Pasqual said grudgingly.

John Colter grinned. "We're about to acquire law and order, Pasqual. Better to be on the side of the law, eh?"

They sold the cattle in Texas and spent two days carousing in a dirty trail town. Buck disappeared with a woman while the others got drunk and played cards; but when the others were inclined to linger, Buck routed them out and led the way west. He took them south around Colter's range, into the dry canyon a mile east of Fort Ellis. In early evening Buck went off toward town, returned an hour later, and led them down to the corral behind Leslie's store. Buck had spent a busy hour, as witnessed by the mattresses and five-gallon cans of coal oil.

"Burn the store," Buck said. "I'll meet you at the pens."

The others hesitated and Bailey said, "Come on." He had spoken very little during the day, showing neither approval nor disregard for Buck's ideas. He knelt beside a mattress and slit one side with his knife; this was more to his liking, this made sense. They owed Charley Leslie a left-handed debt if nothing else. Bailey poured coal oil on the ripped mattress, hauled it aside, and began on the next.

"Ed," Buck said.

"Yes?"

"No shootin' tonight."

Buck caught the nod of agreement and led his horse off south. He made a wide circle to the river and tied the black in the willows above the ford. Then he walked to Glendon's back door and cupped his hands; his soft whistle brought Glendon outside, lamp in hand.

"You make a fine target," Buck laughed softly.

"Buck," Glendon said. "Hold it!"

Glendon disappeared inside and the lamp snuffed out. Glendon called, "Come on in, Buck."

Buck slipped through the doorway, shook hands, and gave Glendon a quick bear hug. Glendon lit a candle and set out cups, put the coffee on, turned two chairs into the table. In the candle's yellow cone Buck's face floated above his dark shirt, thinned and coarsened, whipped by wind and leathered by sun. Buck's smile was wide and cheerful but, like the candle, it gave no true warmth, it was a contrivance of skin and teeth.

"Buck, it's good to see you," Glendon said.

"Surprised?"

"Yes," he said. "I figured you'd be south."

"How far, Pat?"

"With the river between us," Glendon said. "Things are rough around here, Buck."

"It wasn't our fault," Buck said. "You know damn well Colter sent that bunch in."

"I didn't mean that," Glendon said.

"For God sakes," Buck said, completely at a loss. "What else is there, Pat?"

"That boy," Glendon said. "At Colter's south camp."

He waited for a denial, knowing it would be the truth, but Buck only reached for the bubbling pot and poured his coffee and grinned.

"Oh, him?" Buck said. "Hell, I plumb forgot that, Pat. I had no choice, he gave me trouble."

Glendon wanted to ask what trouble an unarmed boy of seventeen could offer five men; and the words were useless. Buck simply would not understand. Buck was gone, gone forever over that line Glendon knew so well.

"A new governor was sworn in," Glendon said. "I hear he's going to take the roof off the territory."

"On account of here," Buck said. "And maybe on account of me?"

"Yes, Buck," he said steadily. "On account of you."

"I knew it," Buck laughed. "I read a couple of them eastern newspapers over in Texas. They sure gave us a big spread, eh?"

"They sure did," Glendon said. "I don't like that, Buck."

"Don't you worry about me," Buck said. "If that governor don't bother me, I'll leave him alone."

"Buck," Glendon said patiently, "that's the point. He can't leave you alone. He's got to do something."

"An' where do you stand, Pat?"

"Where I always did," Glendon said. "I want to see things settled down."

"With old John snorting?" Buck laughed. "And Adams sticking around here? Hell, between them, Pat, they won't let things settle down. That Pasqual is goin' to trail me from now till hell freezes over."

"Maybe the governor can handle Colter," Glendon said.

"Can't be done," Buck said. "But what I stopped in to say was, you want to take a little ride? We're heading for Sherman."

"Ed Bailey?" he asked.

"Ed and some other boys."

"No, Buck," he said steadily. "It wouldn't do any good now."

"Are you figuring on staying here?" Buck asked.

"A while longer," he said. "I—"

He heard the wild yell uptown, "FIRE!" and ran to the front door and saw the first flames rising from Leslie's store. When he turned to grab his bucket Buck put a hand on his arm and grinned.

"If you stay," Buck said, "you'll sure have plenty of building room."

"Buck," he said.

"Pat, I just got to go."

"Buck," he said sharply. "What for?"

"Oh, you mean that?" Buck said. "Calling card for Leslie. Teach the bastard to stay out of other folks' business. Adios, Pat."

In the two weeks following the burning of Leslie's store, business ground almost to a standstill in Fort Ellis. Leslie refused to rebuild, swore he was done with business, yet made no move to leave town. Leslie had received his orders from John Colter and was biding his time, waiting for Adams' next move; and Adams, hauling in supplies and opening a makeshift store in the livery barn, made no move. Every available man worked on the new Adams building, rising now from the cleared wreckage, and Adams directed all work from the tiny barn office. Swift was forced to do bookwork at home; and Glendon dropped by more often than before to help her add figure columns and finish each day's job so they could fish the river.

As the days passed news trickled in from the territory. Buck and his crew were stealing cattle from Colter, taking horses from everybody, slipping into Sherman for supplies

and fandangoes, carrying on an unending war against Cross
C. Buck killed four men during that period, Ed Bailey shot
another, and rumor numbered Buck's crew at ten, then
fifteen, then twenty. On Monday of the third week Joe Jones
came to Glendon's house with a message: the governor's
personal representative would like to speak with him in
Adams' office.

"In a few minutes, Joe," Glendon said.

He finished shaving and slipped on his last outfit of worn,
patched clothes and crossed the back lot, knowing what to
expect, not knowing what to answer. He met the governor's
man, a gentleman of fifty-odd with sharp blue eyes and tiny
white teeth gleaming behind a brown beard. His name was
Avery and he wasted no time getting to business.

"The governor is ready to act," Avery said. "He is mailing
letters to various men throughout the territory. He has pro-
posed an amnesty to all men who have broken the law. If
those men will come to the capitol, put off their guns, and
sign the amnesty, they will not be held liable for any crimes
or killings previous to that date. The governor feels it's the
only way we can wipe the slate clean and start fresh. What
do you think of the idea, Glendon?"

"The governor means well," Glendon said.

"You don't think it will work?"

"It hinges on one thing," Glendon said. "Will every man
concerned take off his guns?"

"That's the rub," Avery said. "We've got our doubts, too,
but we have to try it. If it won't work, the governor will take
immediate steps. He will appoint a sheriff in every county.
We'll go on from there, and I don't have to explain what
happens next. You know the procedure. That brings me to
the real purpose of this visit. If the amnesty fails, will you
accept appointment as sheriff of this county?"

Swift Stamm entered the office with her books, saw their
faces, and stepped back. She said, "Excuse me, I'll wait," but
Adams said, "Come in, Swift. Mrs. Stamm, this is Mr. Avery
from the capitol. Swift is my treasured assistant, Mr. Avery."

"Pleasure, ma'am," Avery said.

He rose to shake hands, gathered his hat from the desk,
and touched Glendon's elbow, moving them both very
smoothly outside into the barn wall shade.

"Well?" he said.

"Try your amnesty," Glendon said. "I promise you an
answer if it fails."

"I have little hope," Avery said. "That is in confidence,

Glendon. And the governor will do almost anything within reason to hire you. Men of your experience are rare as dodo birds."

"Say it the right way," Glendon said brutally. "All the dodo birds are dead."

"Then say it that way," Avery said. "Your kind are few and most of them are dead. We want to hire you. We need you. Is that honest enough?"

"Yes," he said, and then he had to ask, "Who takes Buck's answer to the governor?"

"I will," Avery said. "I'm delivering his letter in person."

Glendon looked again at the round-bellied man. Avery had a deceptive blandness of face and body; then Glendon saw the high-riding shoulder holsters under the thick arms, saw the calluses on Avery's stubby thumbs. Avery might be a stranger to the country but he had traveled. Yes, indeed, Glendon thought, if he didn't smell the mark of a very special former Pinkerton man, then he was blind.

"Good luck to you," Glendon said. "Will you take a suggestion?"

"Gladly."

"Leave your guns in the buggy," Glendon said.

"Thanks," Avery smiled, "but I can handle Buck, I think."

"No," he said. "You're looking at him the wrong way. I don't doubt you can handle him, Avery. Buck's not so fast. I know him well enough to say that. He just shoots, Avery, with no reason. From anywhere."

"I see," Avery said softly. "Thank you, Glendon. I will leave my guns in the buggy . . . this trip."

Glendon watched him pause at the office door to bid Adams good-bye, step into the waiting buggy beside the driver, and swing in a tight circle toward the river. Swift joined him and, walking away, they saw the dust rise high behind those flying wheels. The governor was an unknown man, sitting far away, but Avery proved one fact beyond doubt: this territory would change if it meant calling on Federal troops.

"Did he ask you?" she said.

"Yes," Glendon said. "Let them try the amnesty dodge first."

"You don't know what to answer," she said. "I know that, Pat. And it's not the money. You don't care about the money or the position."'

No, he thought, he could truthfully say he had never placed the almighty dollar first; or the privileges of the position in which too many of his breed grew pompous and overbearing. It went beyond money and privilege, even past the satisfaction of doing a job to the best of his ability. It grew into the good feeling that came from maintaining an orderly town, a clean county, filled with people who could walk unafraid. A man remembered that part long after his nerve dissolved and his time was overdue. And now in this new town, in this strange land, he had watched people walk in fear day and night. These dark-eyed, gentle people had placed an unfair burden on his thoughts. He liked them, he was getting the feel of the country, and most of all he was responding against his better judgment to the old, instinctive responses Avery had ignited.

"Swift," he said, "it'll be a few days. Maybe we ought to think about ourselves."

"We?" she said.

"If I stay on," he said, "it's because of these poor damned people. They need help, any kind they can beg or borrow. But that's not all. I'm wondering about you and me."

"So am I," Swift Stamm said honestly. "Pat, I don't know what to say."

"Not now," he said quickly.

He lengthened his stride and left her, thinking that he might have queered everything. But he wanted her to understand it was no moonstruck foolishness; it could be a fine thing for them if they both broke from their pasts and saw the future together as something possible, something to work toward and hold.

Avery returned on the fifth day, crossed the river, and drove directly to Glendon's house. He got down, much the worse for wear, and shook hands gravely.

"Take it up to the barn," Avery told his driver. "I'll walk over."

Then Avery turned and walked inside without invitation, seated himself at the kitchen table, and shook his head.

"I don't know about the other letters," Avery said. "But I still have Buck's."

"You see him?" Glendon asked.

"Could you make some coffee?"

"Yes," he said. "Basin's over there if you want to wash."

He made coffee while Avery washed face and hands; before the pot boiled Avery lit a cigar and began talking, choosing his words with care.

"I can speak frankly with you, I think. I have been around a bit, as you have guessed by now, and seen my share of

tough customers. This one has me stumped. Yes, I saw Buck.
We got into Sherman the afternoon after we left here. I went
into Smith's saloon and inquired for Buck, and Smith pointed
to the back table. I introduced myself, he shook hands with a
big grin, and invited me to sit down. One minute we were
alone, next a man named Bailey was sitting with us and three
more were out front watching my driver. I gave Buck the
governor's letter. He read it twice and told me it wouldn't
work. Can you guess why not?"

"Here," Glendon said, pouring the coffee. "Yes, some of it.
He told you it would be fine to take off his guns if all the
Cross C outfit took off theirs, and all the other people Buck's
rubbed the wrong way. He told you if he signed that amnesty
and took off his guns, he was good as dead because any one
of fifty men would shoot him the first chance they got."

"You know him pretty well," Avery said. "He gave me all
those reasons and a few more. He and Bailey feel that
Adams wants to get rid of them because they'd worked for
McMann. Buck refused to sign. Nor would he promise to
leave the territory when I suggested it might be wise for all
concerned. I offered him a week's grace to reconsider, to
wire the governor if he changed his mind. I don't expect
that, Glendon."

"Was he staying in Sherman?" Glendon asked.

"Evidently he was in no hurry."

"If you think it'll help," Glendon said, "I'll ride up and talk
with him."

"That's a generous offer," Avery said. "I know how you
happened to meet Buck. He told me all about it. I'd say he
likes you better than any man he has ever known. Strange,
on such short acquaintance, but it happens. You could talk
yourself blue in the face and it wouldn't help. He's past
redemption, Glendon, and we both know it. He smiles and
there's nothing behind the smile. He is probably the most
dangerous man I have ever met. Glendon, let's not beat
around the bush. Will you accept the appointment?"

"You know what I ought to do," Glendon said.

"Of course," Avery said quietly. "Get on your horse and
head for California. But you won't. You're as incorrigible as
I am. Look at me, Glendon! More years than I care to
remember in the agency, retired last year. Along comes an
old friend, a general with whom I served. He's taking a new
post and he needs help. I don't need the money or the
mountain air, but I'm on a train in two days. Why? Tell me
why, Glendon? I know all about you, and I like everything I

heard. I know why you resigned and rode away, and I don't blame you. Every man has a limit. But did you ever think that we are the same breed, always looking hopefully for the same things, the better things? I hope to find them in this new country. I'm just fool enough to believe that I can help make this territory a good place to live. That's the selfish part of every man, of course, for what we really want is a good place for ourselves. So we fight and bleed to make a good place on earth, just for ourselves, and end up helping others. Like these people out here, Glendon, who had three friends killed the other night, not wanting trouble, just trying to make the town a better place. You can't dodge it, Glendon. Either you'll pack up and ride away in an hour, or you'll stay on. And if you stay, you've got to help us. A man does only a few tasks well. Some of us are limited to one. What we do well, we have got to do. Glendon, I'm asking a great deal—perhaps your life—and I'm just selfish enough to demand it. Will you take this appointment?"

Avery placed the stiff, official paper on the table between them. Avery had spoken words that rang true, fired both barrels with telling effect. Glendon had used the same argument he had given young deputies in past years—oh, not the same words, for he could not talk that well, but he had slapped it into those young men and rarely had he failed. And when he did fail, he knew he was lucky, for he did not want such a man guarding his back.

Avery knew him too well. A man could not ride away from his past; it colored all his future and made him a puppet, helpless before his own instincts. He unfolded the paper and read the official wordage and noted the salary—an unreasonably high rate of pay—and felt the pencil pushed into his right hand.

"We don't need ink," Avery said.

He signed and watched Avery replace the paper in his coat and lay the star on the table: it glittered in the dull light, shone into his eyes.

"Now," Avery said. "You need two deputies. Any preferences?"

"None," he said.

"I have two recommendations," Avery said. "Charley Leslie, who has good reason to volunteer. He recommended another man, Jones at the livery barn. Jones has other reasons. He wants a better job with higher pay, but I think he can handle it. Will you go along with them at the start?"

"They'll do," he said.

"I'll appoint them immediately," Avery said. "Now what do you need?"

Now the past came pressing down, and he thought of Buck. Swift would know within the day, but he could not change his methods. She wanted him to take the job; now she had to understand.

"A shotgun," he said flatly. "Ten-gauge double-barrel, sawed off two inches past the forearm. Case of double-ought buckshot. Colt and Winchester ammunition. Same order for both deputies."

"Within a week," Avery said. "Perhaps you didn't know it, but the county seat has been in a small town to the west. The governor is changing it to Fort Ellis for several good reasons. Before I leave, I will start construction of a courthouse with offices and a jail. Glendon, you take orders only from the governor, or from me through him. Call on me at any time. That's what I'm for."

"When you talked with Buck," Glendon said, "did you tell him about me?"

"You mean, who you really are?"

"Yes."

"It was plain he didn't know," Avery said. "I held my tongue. He'll hear the news soon enough."

"Yes," he said. "Buck will hear the news."

They had come down from the northeast at dawn, eaten breakfast, and slept through the heat of the day. The town was quiet and no one disturbed them, not even the handsome young man with the game leg who drove his wagon toward the river and the hills beyond. But during the day a man rode into town and talked with Coyote Smith, and rode on his way. Coyote Smith polished glasses and waited expectantly for suppertime. When Buck and Ed Bailey came up the back hall and lifted their pre-supper drinks, Smith said idly, "Heard some news today."

"What?" Ed Bailey said. "The governor drop dead?"

"Not exactly," Smith said. "He appointed a new sheriff in this county."

Buck said carelessly, "We'll keep him busy appointing new sheriffs. Who is it, Coyote? Some potgut from the capitol?"

"Why no," Smith said. "A man from Fort Ellis named Glendon."

Buck tossed off his drink and rolled a cigaret, his face round and pleasantly blank. Finally he said, "Pat Glendon?"

"That's the man," Smith said. "They're building a new

courthouse in Ellis, complete with jail and handcuffs. An' he's got two deputies, man named Leslie and another one named Jones."

"Pat Glendon," Buck said. "Not old Pat."

"That ain't what they called him up in Kansas," Smith said. "Up there they called him 'Shotgun' Glendon, and I guess we don't need no diagram to tell us why."

"If he comes through here," Buck said, "tell him to stay out of my way. Leslie and Jones! That goddamn Leslie and his store, now he's after trouble too. Tell them I start shooting on sight. You hear me, Coyote? Tell him to stay clear."

"You sort of liked him, eh?" Coyote Smith said.

"Just pour the whisky, you sonofabitch," Buck said tonelessly. "I've got no friends. I don't need any!"

Chapter Five

GLENDON ESTABLISHED a temporary office in the harness shop across the street from the livery barn. That same day workmen poured into town, pegged down a tent camp, and began the courthouse in the vacant lot just above Leslie's burned-out store. Later in the morning the southbound stage brought Glendon a sealed pouch from the governor's office; and minutes later a fast freight wagon deposited a packing case outside the livery barn. Jones went over, read the shipping tag, and signaled.

"For you, Pat."

Glendon saw Swift come from Adams' desk and watch as Jones ripped off the top boards with a crowbar. He wanted to hold off until she went home, but that was splitting hairs. She would see the evidence of his past soon enough. Charley Leslie followed him across the street and helped Jones lift three stiff cardboard gun boxes from the packing case. Glendon opened the top box, stripped away the oiled paper, and held the double-barrel ten-gauge in his hands. Avery had sent the very best, three English Greeners. An unknown gunsmith had cut the barrels and filed the raw edges smooth; the hammers clicked evenly under his thumb, trigger pull was steady behind his forefinger. *A trifle heavy,* experience whispered; *have to ease them off a bit.* Then he looked up and met Swift's eyes. He had warned her fairly, but the shock was plain.

"Now, by God," Jones said. "We're in business."

"Cart the ammunition over," Glendon said. "Clean the guns. Break out a box of shells each. Target practice in ten minutes."

"With this?" Jones laughed. "We don't need practice with a cannon."

"Ten minutes," he said. "Up the hill behind Leslie's corral."

"Pat," Jones said. "It's hot!"

"How much do you know about this gauge?" he asked.

"I've shot twelves," Jones said. "There's no difference."

"At what?" he said. "Ducks, rabbits?"

"Sure."

"You won't be shooting ducks," Glendon said coldly. "So get acquainted."

He waited until they carried the packing case across the street; he took Swift's arm and led her away from the office door and tried a smile that failed. She bumped the sawed-off barrels and flinched, and Glendon said, "It won't bite, Swift."

"Pat," she said. "I didn't—"

"Heft it," he said. "Go on, smell it!"

He laid the shotgun in her hands and felt her arms give beneath the weight. Grease smudged her fingers, she looked reluctantly at the blue barrel sheen, at the plain walnut stock lacking the usual high polish.

"Dull," she said. "Ugly."

"Dull for a reason," Glendon said. "You want no sunlight flashing, giving away your position. There's always a reason, Swift. I've had a dozen of these. Get used to it. I hope I'll never use it on anything but rabbits, but I'll tell you this—it's my last one, win, lose, or draw."

"So heavy," she said.

Glendon broke the shell box and spilled two into his left hand. He breeched the shotgun, reamed grease from the chambers with his little finger, and inserted the shells. Their brass faces glinted in the sun; the primers were round copper nipples buried in the brass. He unloaded and the gun slipped under his arm in a natural motion.

"Has to be heavy," he said. "To carry these loads. Swift, I wanted you to see it. I took the job, now I'm tied to it. From now on you'll be doing the fishing for both of us."

"I know," she said, "but we can have coffee at night."

"With luck," he said. "Now get out of this sun."

She smiled and walked away, leaving him alone in the barn wall shade, the smell of grease and oil rising thick in his nostrils. He thought of bygone days when he patrolled his street—and it was always his street—with the shotgun under his arm; it had become a symbol in those towns, a mark of rough justice. Glendon turned across the street and, from

Adams's new building, workmen watched him furtively. It was always that way; now they expected miracles. He stepped inside the tiny office, lifted a cleaning rod from the packing case, and took his chair behind the desk.

"Get some rags, Joe," he said. "Soft, clean ones."

"Where?" Jones said.

"Get them," he said. "Stop wasting time."

For time would pass like magic from this day forward. He had to train Jones and Leslie, but there was never time to train them thoroughly. He had the firm promise of six additional men when he needed a posse, but such men were forever making mistakes. In the letter pouch on the table was the beginning of the end for Buck: blank warrants, handcuffs, a note from Avery telling him to go ahead. Well, give Buck a little more time and he'd go ahead. It was only a matter of time.

"All right," he said. "Let's go up the hill."

The coffee tasted flat in her mouth and she could not eat the slice of cake. Swift Stamm sat at her kitchen table and saw the familiar door-sized rectangle of green trees and river to the west. On too many endless days, sitting here, that narrow doorful of greenery seemed to represent all she knew of earth and life. The feel of the shotgun was still on her hands; the brown grease was ingrained in her fingernails. So, she thought, she had practically begged him to take the job, to stay; and here he was, as she wished. But that wasn't altogether true. Something else had held him at the last moment, something out of his past, for what else was his compulsion but the unbreakable habit of a past she feared? He'd go out and do his job, as she wished, and now *she* faced a job. No one could help her, either; like Pat, she walked alone. She wanted love, and she was afraid.

A strange romance, she thought bitterly. Sitting on a river bank, drinking coffee, eating cake, talking of this and that— and what did people really mean when they said "This and that?" She was too old for all the pleasures of young love, the new dress, the flowers, the buggy ride in the moonlight. All that was dried out and hung on the clothesline of spent years. Were those happy pieces of youth the "this and that"? Did all that come just once and then vanish? She had only unhappy memories of Stamm—failure in Kansas, moving on through alien country, life in Fort Ellis, the slow, painful knowledge that Stamm was no better than McMann and Adams. To come from that life at Stamm's death and live alone for two years had been a great blessing; and now she had met a man who seemed different.

Who *was* different, she corrected herself angrily. Now she was doubting herself, thinking dishonestly. She drew back from love but she wanted it all to come again, dear God how she wanted it, and the past had coated her with a callous of distrust for all men. She wanted to feel love for Glendon, and all she could muster up in her heart was security and a sense of warm companionship, of finding someone who believed in her. Was that enough, was that the final answer to loneliness? She wanted it all once more and she dared not make a mistake; she wanted no half loaf. But doubt spoke softly, *A half loaf is better than none*.

"Damn it," she said. "Damn it all to hell!"

July wore on and August came with unabated heat. Black clouds rolled falsely above the peaks, lightning flashed in the night sky, rain was only a mirage. Glendon trained his deputies and rode out on the lonely trails and drew into his mind a picture of his country. He sat in the stuffy office and waited through the long, hot days for the first break, the word from Avery, the time to start. He watched the building race between Adams' local crew and the capitol workgang. The new hotel took on shape, the courthouse rose from foundations to walls and finally rafters. Adams' crew built with adobe and vigas and rough-cut lumber; the workgang built the courthouse from timbers and boards, every sliver hauled down from the railroad siding. The courthouse was no Grecian urn, no thing of beauty forever; it was a stopgap built for one purpose—to place a mantle of authority over the county.

The authority was centered in two spots: cells and courtroom. Railroad ties went into the cell block walls, with casehardened steel in bars and doors and locks. The courtroom was stark simplicity, double doors opening into a center aisle flanked by straight-backed seats, the jury box down front on the left, the judge's desk and high chair on a raised dais in front. The right-hand door led into the sheriff's office; an inner door gave access to the cells. Glendon moved into the office an hour after the last nail was hammered home; and across the street Adams' crew finished the hotel roof and puttied the big windows into the bar front. The same bartender tapped his first keg of beer and broached his whisky; that night was Adams' grand opening, with everything on the house.

Adams had no beds in his hotel, no counter in his cafe, no desk in his new upstairs office; but he played the host that night, he rushed the growler with a smile, and the town whooped it up as men had laughed and sung and drunk in McMann's time. That same night a special messenger brought the latest news on Buck, a stack of Eastern papers with a letter from Avery.

Buck's gang had grown to eight members, all men who ignored the governor's amnesty and wanted only to live their own lives at the expense of others, work not, yet reap all the harvests. The papers were filled with overblown accounts of Buck's adventures. The legend was started and only time would dull the sharp edge. One story in particular grated on Glendon's nerves as he read that night in his new office.

It told how Buck was a friend of all the natives in the territory, how he rode for days without danger, stopping at the simple huts of Mexican friends. Robin Hood was riding again. Yes, Buck stopped wherever he pleased, and why not? Fear rode with him, fear that turned a poor man's heart to jelly. And yet another story about the woman Buck loved, how he was faithful to her, how he dared all the mighty power of the law to spend a few minutes at her side. They even had her name correct—Juanita Lopez—but no mention of her legal husband. Nor did they write of twenty other women in twenty other houses where Buck spread his favors with a glad hand. And then the scoreboard; oh yes, that was common knowledge too. The last paper in the stack, dated ten days ago, had Buck's grand total marked at thirteen and insinuated that each man of that baker's dozen was a scoundrel who deserved to die.

Avery wrote that Buck was growing bolder as the weeks passed, laughing at authority because no one stood in his way. Avery suggested that Glendon go himself, or send a man, to map the town of Sherman, that Buck returned there from every ride. Very soon, Avery wrote, they would get the opening they needed, the break that counted, and then it might well come to an ending in that town. Glendon read the letter twice, lit a match, and watched the paper burn to a gray ash. When Jones came from the bar party, smelling of whisky and foolish talk, Glendon closed the door and said, "You sober?"

"I'm all right," Jones said. "Just a few drinks."

Jones and Leslie were champing at the bit, eager to start, to use their newly acquired authority. Jones might turn out fine, but Leslie was hurting himself with his burning hatred for Buck. Therefore he would send Jones on this first important assignment.

"You start tonight," Glendon said. "Ride up to Sherman. I want the name of every man riding with Buck. I want a map of Sherman, every street and building and shed, distances from the town to the river and surrounding hills, all roads leading out of town. I want the location of one house double-checked—a family named Lopez, the wife's name is Juanita. I don't care how you get it, but be back a week from tonight. Leave the shotgun, wear your badge inside your shirt."

"Alone?" Jones said.

"You need help on a simple job?"

Jones reddened and tossed his cigaret into the spittoon. He made a great show of collecting his gear, taking ammunition from the case. Glendon said quietly, "I wouldn't send you, Joe, if I didn't think you could handle the job," and walked from the office before Jones became thoroughly embarrassed. He passed the saloon and moved deeper down the dark street; and Adams spoke to him from the unfinished windows fronting the cafe.

"Busy, Pat?"

"Always busy," he said. "Good party you're giving."

"The boys worked hard," Adams said. "They earned it. Pat, what are you waiting on?"

He wanted to believe that Adams had changed, that the past was forgotten and Adams sincerely wanted a new way of life in Fort Ellis. But Adams had not changed; and he could name the biggest reason. He was silent with his thoughts and Adams said again, "Buck's running wild, Pat. What are you waiting on?"

"You," he said. "Someone like you, Adams."

"Me?" Adams said. "You're the law, Pat."

"You're the citizen," Glendon said. "Will you sign a complaint, give evidence? Come over now, Adams. Sign a complaint against Buck and I'll start tonight."

"But—"

"Yes," he said softly. "But what?"

He walked away through the night, around the livery barn, and saw darkness where Swift's house lay. He wished that lamp was on. They should sit together and talk, and tonight might be his last chance. Avery's letter tolled the end of marking time.

Buck, he thought sadly, why don't you ride south and keep riding until the river is behind you?

Ed Bailey leaned forward in the saddle and stretched his aching muscles. They were sticking leather for the tenth hour, killing their horses, running from the failure south of Las Vegas. Buck had gotten the idea of giving Colter a rest, going north and trying the ranches above the railroad. Buck never thought out a plan, he just acted, and they had experienced the taste of trying their luck on strange ground.

They rode into a line camp under a rimrock, where a rock cabin guarded corrals and windmill and pens; and the man inside called one warning and began shooting. He killed Duffy and drove them off to the south; but Buck had reached the stage where he wouldn't turn from the devil himself. Buck pushed them up on a line and tried to kill a man hidden behind foot-thick rocks; and only when half a dozen rifles opened on them from the rimrock above the cabin did Buck pull out. They had ridden ten hours and were near the railroad now, but it was fifty long miles to Sherman. Ed Bailey rubbed his cramped stomach muscles and felt his horse quiver between his legs. They had to get fresh horses or rest.

Last man to top the ridge, Bailey saw the lights marking the telegraph station on the main line. A month ago one operator handled that key and took care of the switch track; now building supplies were unloaded daily and freighted south to Fort Ellis, and someone had passed the word that surveyors were almost ready to lay out a branch line through Fort Ellis to the Texas border. A smart man would give this place a wide berth, but Buck took them straight down the last slope toward the depot light.

The signal tower arms were straight up, yellow lamp glow colored the dormer windows, shining on the worn desk and the operator's key and sounder. Buck got down and walked to the nearest corral calling, "In here, boys. Let's swap."

Then the door opened and the operator stepped outside, holding a lantern above his head. Ed Bailey wanted to shout at him, tell him to stay inside, but it was too late. The operator saw Buck enter the corral and ran forward with an angry shout, "Get out of there!" He reached the gate as Buck came leading a horse, he grabbed for the halter and Buck gave him a push that sent him flat on his backside.

"Stop," he said. "Those horses are railroad property!"

The operator scrambled to his feet and started for Buck. Ed Bailey turned his head and looked at the sky; but the stars did not deaden the shot. Then Buck called sharply, "Hurry it up!"

Bailey ran around Buck into the corral. As the others followed, he picked a horse, led it outside and changed his saddle and bridle. Down the switch track in a bunk boxcar someone yelled, other men answered, and Buck came from the depot on the run. They mounted and swung away into darkness with the angry shouts growing in volume.

"They'll send no wires," Buck laughed. "Anyway, not for awhile."

Bailey remembered Buck talking a few days ago, wondering aloud why Glendon hadn't made a move. That was over now. Buck had killed the wrong man, and Glendon would move for sure.

"Buck," he said. "Where to?"

"Sherman," Buck said. "She's the nearest, ain't she?"

"Juanita?" Bailey said.

"Who else?" Buck laughed. "We need a little fun."

Bailey wanted to say, "Let's hit for the border," and held his tongue. But not much longer, he thought. Buck could go on acting the fool. He was getting out.

John Colter rode into Fort Ellis with thirty men behind him. They spread along the street while Colter walked up the steps into the new courthouse and ambled down the center aisle toward the sheriff's office. Pasqual followed him closely, and two men took stations outside the double doors. John Colter entered the office, grinned at Charley Leslie and Glendon, and dropped into the nearest chair.

"Pat," John Colter said. "Here you got a new courthouse and deputies, an' you ain't done nothing for a month. When are you taking Buck off my back?"

Colter always used the blunt approach on a man. He enjoyed dropping hot words in a man's lap and watching him squirm; and he was disappointed when Glendon regarded him with absolutely no surprise.

"Waiting on you," Glendon said.

"On me?"

"Swear out your complaints," Glendon said. "Name your witnesses. We'll do the rest."

"Complaints?" Colter said. "Hell, you know what's going on. Buck killed my foreman, and that boy in the south camp. Go out and get him. Bring him home in a box."

Glendon inked a pen in the bottle and looked up calmly. "Get it down, Colter. Are your witnesses ready to testify in court?"

John Colter held his angry words. He had made no headway at the capitol. The governor was backing Glendon to the limit and had passed the word that he expected one hundred percent cooperation from every rancher in the territory. John Colter dared not sign that complaint, name his witnesses. If Glendon brought Buck alive to trial, a real honest-to-god trial with judge, jury, and honest lawyers, Buck might talk loud and long about the days he had worked for Cross C. Then too, Buck had been in Texas the past month; and fifteen men already paid off were too many to keep shut-mouthed forever. John Colter had come to test Glendon, and he wasted no time in judging a man.

"We're in a heluva shape," he said testily, "when an honest man can't get justice. I guess if you're just goin' to squat on your hands, I'll do something myself."

He stomped out of the courthouse and cooled his heels on the steps. He waited patiently until Charley Leslie stood beside him, and then he said, "What's going on?"

"Jones is scouting Sherman," Charley Leslie said softly. "We were just making plans when you came in. I'm going up there tonight."

"What for?"

"Help Jones."

"God damn it," John Colter said. "That don't tell me nothing."

"That's all I know," Leslie said. "Don't be so impatient."

"So?" John Colter said shrewdly. "Feeling your oats."

"Doing my job," Leslie said meaningly. "And getting paid in cash."

"You'll be paid," Colter said. "Just keep your eyes open. Watch Adams, get word to me through Manuel."

"Paid?" Leslie said pointedly. "Just when, Mr. Colter?"

"That was my store burned," Colter growled. "I lost the money. Keep your shirt on."

"When?" Leslie repeated. "You are one month behind. If you want news, I want last month's pay in cash this afternoon."

"How much?"

"Five hundred," Leslie said. "From now on."

"FIVE—!"

"I'm risking my life," Leslie said. "Ante up or the deal is off."

John Colter had been ready to give further instructions: namely, Buck must not be taken alive. Now he turned and glared at Leslie and changed his entire course of action. No man had ever forced him; no man ever would.

"You tinhorn," John Colter said. "Let me say it for you—our deal is off. And don't go peddling certain information or you'll leave this town in a box." He turned and touched Pasqual on the arm. "Take a good look at him, Pasqual."

"I see him, patron," Pasqual said.

"Save it for the peons," Charley Leslie said coldly. "You promise a lot, Colter, and you pay off in pennies. Now stop trying to bribe an officer of the law or I'll step inside and report to Glendon."

John Colter had his temper under control once more; he grinned, hitched up his overalls, and went down the street to the new hotel. C. B. Adams, superintending the placement of the cafe counter, greeted him pleasantly, glanced toward the courthouse, and offered a deliberate wink.

"Seeing our new sheriff, Mr. Colter?"

John Colter stepped through the empty door casing and motioned Adams into a corner. "You figure on doing business the same way, Adams?"

"I had no fire sale," Adams said, "but I'm back at the old stand."

"You'll get burned out again," Colter said bluntly.

"Oh, come now," Adams said. "Those days are finished. Our new sheriff is unbribable, Mr. Colter. You should know, eh? You just saw him."

"You going to keep those beef contracts?" Colter said.

"I have certain leads," Adams said primly. "And a bit of influence."

"Penny ante," Colter said scornfully. "And you'll buy no more of my cattle, Adams. I've got my craw full and I'm all done fiddling around. I'm going to Washington next week and take a closer look at your influence."

"Do that," Adams said. "Although I doubt your reason for the trip. I think perhaps you want to be a healthy distance from Fort Ellis if Glendon brings Buck in."

"If I go to Washington because of Buck," John Colter said shrewdly, "you ought to head for South America."

"Then why are we at odds?" Adams said softly. "We want the same thing, Mr. Colter. I'm thinking of the future when this country opens up. If I were a palm-reader, a fortune teller, I might say, 'I see you selling cattle to me, I see myself selling those herds to the government. I see all concerned making more money and staying within the law.' Well?"

John Colter said swiftly, "Can you take care of Buck?"

"I can," Adams said. "Given time."

"Then take care of him," Colter said bluntly, "and we'll talk business."

"In my own way, no questions asked?"

"No questions asked."

Charley Leslie did not ride alone that night. A messenger came roaring down from the railroad, Glendon read Avery's terse note, and sent for Leslie and all posse members. They were mounted and riding within thirty minutes, Manuel leading them north in a steady driving pace. They rode through the night and camped in timber five miles south of Sherman the next morning. At that time, breakfast hastily cooked and eaten, Glendon sent Manuel forward to scout the town and locate Jones.

Manuel took the open road and came boldly into Sherman, dismounted outside the saloon, and limped inside. He saw Jones at a table, playing cooncan with a harmless looking old man, and decided to bluff it straight through. Manuel had a drink, questioned Coyote Smith about work, and took his leave. He trotted south over the first ridge, waited patiently, and a few minutes later Jones came on the trot. Manuel said, "Follow me," and led Jones back to the river camp. Jones went straight to the breakfast fire and squatted beside Glendon.

"Here's the names," Jones said, opening his notebook. "That one scratched out—he's dead up at Vegas."

"Did they come in night before last?" Glendon asked.

"Seven of 'em," Jones said. "Stayed all night and hung around till last night when a Mex came down from the north and passed them some news. They headed west right after dark."

"You know why they left?"

"Oh, sure," Jones said. "The news was all over town this morning."

"How do these people take it?"

"Listen," Jones said, "they're scared to death of him."

"Think they'd help him?"

"No," Jones said thoughtfully. "They're just standing by."

"Lay out your map."

Jones spread his rough pencil sketch on the ground. The others gathered around and Jones pointed out roads, plaza, old army buildings, and the Lopez house. He described all roads, each one as far as he had been able to ride out. His work was good and he accepted Glendon's thanks with a self-conscious grunt.

"Now what?" he said.

"We start the merry-go-round," Glendon said. "We get them quick or we keep trying. We'll try that west road first. Leslie, you take everybody a mile out that west road from the river. Find the best place for shooting and square off. Manuel, you keep covering the other roads."

"Si."

"Jones," Glendon said, "you come with us. We're going into town."

"Town?" Jones said.

"I want to get acquainted," Glendon said. "Hang around all day and leave tonight for home."

"But we don't go home, eh?"

"It's an old dodge," Glendon said. "Worth trying once. Leslie, look for us at dark."

Charley Leslie had learned a great deal about the new sheriff in one month's time. Glendon had taught him the sudden death in a ten-gauge shotgun, a good many tricks of the trade Leslie had never known before; but most of all, Charley Leslie had learned to respect and fear the man he unconsciously thought of now as "Shotgun" Glendon. Charley Leslie had ridden with his violent anger at all the world through the night and into morning. He had come down from the north with the promise of big money dangling just before his eyes, like the carrot on the stick, and now he had nothing left. Colter had booted him out; Adams had offered him nothing concrete. All he had was a rage that centered entirely on Buck. Buck was the cause of everything, and Charley Leslie would follow Glendon to hell for a chance at Buck.

"Whistle twice," he said. "We'll be ready."

Ed Bailey mounted guard on the hilltop through the day, watching the trail drop down toward Sherman. They were in the high slopes fifteen miles west of town, using a sheepherder's cabin Bailey had discovered a year ago. It was a good spot to rest but absence of pursuit worried Bailey. He recognized the truth Buck had chosen to ignore: the territory was up in arms.

At sundown Bailey came off the hilltop to eat supper. Buck had slept all day, indifferent to danger, and now Buck made his plans known.

"Shorty," Buck said. "You and Mac start for town."

McMillan said, "Back to Sherman?"

"Why, sure," Buck smiled. "Rest of us'll tail along behind you."

"Buck," McMillan said. "Maybe we ought to wait another day."

"Tonight," Buck said shortly.

McMillan glanced at Bailey and found no backing. He went through the trees to the horses, pulled his stake, and came down to the tank in the rocks. There was no future in arguing with Buck; not when Buck wanted to see that woman tonight. McMillan led out with Shorty and before they rode a mile forgot most of his fear. He had ridden free so long it was deep in his blood. Maybe Buck was right when he said this country was theirs. But following, half a mile behind, Ed Bailey spoke his mind.

"It ain't the woman, is it?" he asked.

"She'll do," Buck said.

"Plenty of others," Bailey said. "I was thinking we ought to go south a while."

"Go on," Buck said. "Nobody's stopping you."

"Oh hell," Bailey said wearily. "I wonder if Smith'll ever get a different keg of whisky."

Buck laughed and slapped Bailey's shoulder as they rode. "Stop worrying," Buck said. "Sherman's our town. Nobody's got the guts to come in there."

"Not even Glendon?"

"Pat's one man," Buck said. "If he comes up to Sherman, the governor'll need a new sheriff."

"He's a good man," Bailey said softly.

"Sure he's a good man," Buck said. "Don't you think I know it, Ed? I don't want to hurt Pat, but what can I do?"

"Yes," Bailey said. "What can we do?"

Glendon rose from the saloon table at dusk and paid the bill. Coyote Smith followed him to the hitch rail where Jones stood beside the horses. "Glad to have you, Sheriff," Smith said. "Come back any time."

"We'll be back," Glendon said.

"Heading for Fort Ellis?"

"Possibly," Glendon said. "You might do two favors for me, Smith."

"Name them."

"Tell Buck I was here," Glendon said. "Tell him we'll save time and bother if he turns himself in."

"I'll tell him you stopped by," Coyote Smith said. "But not the rest. I'm strictly neutral, Sheriff."

"You are not neutral," Glendon said. "Buck comes and goes in your town, and you have not reported that fact to the authorities. As of today, you are not neutral."

"Matter of opinion," Smith said calmly. "What was the other favor you wanted, Sheriff?"

"I just told you," Glendon said. "You are no longer neutral. Think it over, Smith."

He led Jones south across the plaza onto the south road, followed it two miles, stopped to listen, and made the western circle across the river back to the west road. They came up slowly and saw the thin line of trees along the road. Glendon whistled twice and waited until Leslie called, "Come on in, Pat," and loomed out of the darkness to lead the way to the pickets.

Horses staked, Glendon walked the tree line with Jones, checked every man, placed Leslie at the west end with Jones and went down to take up the flankman's spot on the east. He found a spot ten steps from the road and settled himself against a tree with the shotgun across his knees.

Now the waiting was on him, no different from other times long ago. You waited in the night for the sound of hoofs, voices, and the pattern never varied. If luck smiled, you had a chance. If no one came, you tried another time. The rough cottonwood bark rasped against his back, he smelled his own sweat and thought of Buck, the way Buck's mind worked. Buck had no respect for life; he would sacrifice every man to ride free. Glendon cupped his hands and called to the next man.

"Pass the word," he said. "If one or two come riding, let them go. Understand?"

"Got it . . . ho, Billy!"

The order was relayed up the line to Jones and Leslie. Glendon knew he should have given that order ten minutes ago. Was he getting careless, forgetting that little things meant so much? He shivered in the cooling night and slipped the shotgun higher on his knees; and heard the horses coming from the west.

He went flat and brought the shotgun to bear on the road. He listened to the hoofbeats—two or three horses, no, just two—and lay unmoving as they passed by and disappeared in the moonless night. He counted off the minutes, five, eight, ten, and heard the faint, growing sound of more horses coming leisurely from the west. When the lead rider loomed up in the darkness, ten yards up the road, Glendon cocked his triggers and lifted his voice in a shout.

"Buck, put up your hands!"

He saw the shadowy bulk of horsemen pull close together, then spring apart as spurs drove home. He fired one barrel high against that dissolving mass, closed his eyes as the others began shooting and muzzle blast came red. He looked once more and saw two riders veering off to the north; and far down the road toward town he heard more shots. Then he ran for the road, shouting to Leslie and Jones, "Close in!" and stumbled over a horse. He fell full length, scrambled to his feet, and almost immediately struck a fallen man. He bent down, touched that body, and went on. Ten steps away someone grabbed a bridle rein and tried to soothe a wounded, struggling horse.

"How many?" he said.

"One here," Jones said. "Hold on, here's another one—Pat, this one's alive."

"Watch him," Glendon said.

That made three down, he thought, and two away clear. Two had ridden past. Seven in all; it tallied out. He winced at the horse's high, almost human cry of pain and called, "Shoot it," and stumbled up the road until he found Jones and Leslie beside the wounded man. He said, "Look at the others, Jones," and cupped a match above the face blob. Strange eyes looked up at him, glazed with shock, seeing nothing, or looking far beyond their own vision. Jones came on the run to say, "Both dead, don't know either."

"Get the horses," Glendon said. "Send a man back for Manuel."

"What about this one?" Leslie asked.

"Forget him," Glendon said harshly. "He's gone now."

He cursed savagely, the first time Charley Leslie had felt the axe edge of his temper. "Die on me," Glendon said to the dead man. "When I needed you!" He swung around, bumping Leslie roughly. "Come on, there's no time."

Buck spurred north when he heard Glendon's shout, pulled Ed Bailey along as they left the road, and heard Ed grunt with sudden pain. "Stay up," Buck said, and spurred viciously, getting distance before he chanced a closer look at Ed. If Ed was a goner, well, his horse was still sound. Buck rode a mile, swinging back to the west, pulled both horses to a walk and carefully felt Ed all over.

"High up in the shoulder," Buck said. "You can make it."

"Where?" Bailey said weakly.

"West," Buck said. "They can't trail us at night."

"Not west," Bailey said. "North, Buck. Head north."

"I'm crossing no railroads," Buck said. "Shut up an' ride."

He shunted both horses off to the west, then south until they struck the trail. Bailey tried to talk and gave up, having just enough strength to stick in the saddle. Buck pushed along fast for two miles, then held a slower pace that brought them out of the valley into the ridges, around the conical hill and down the path to the cabin. Bailey fell off before Buck could grab him, struggled to his knees, and crawled toward the cabin. Buck led both horses out back, tied them, and stopped at the tank for a drink. He heard Ed calling, "Water, Buck," and answered, "Keep your shirt on." When he reached the cabin, Ed was flat on his back. He lifted Ed up and held the canteen and let Ed drink his fill.

"Let's take a look at it," Buck said.

"Dust," Bailey said weakly. "You—"

"Shut up," Buck said. "You losin' your mind? It ain't that bad."

"Keep going," Bailey said. "Got to—"

"God damn it!" Buck said. "Will you lay still? Nobody's goin' to trail us tonight. We'll be long gone come morning."

Manuel Martinez and the man sent back to find him caught them no more than a mile up the road. Manuel said, "I met the first two at the river, Sheriff."

"What luck?" he asked.

"One dead," Manuel said. "I tied the other one. He will keep."

"Take over," Glendon said. "Two of them broke north. Maybe they swung west again. You know this country?"

"Very well," Manuel said. "I think they were camped in the hills, there is a cabin up there. Let me go ahead, Senor Glendon. If they circled back to the road I will smell their dust."

"Go," he said.

Manuel took the lead and Glendon followed, at a walk, until Manuel's voice drifted back: "Senor, they came this way."

"You're sure?" he called.

"Very sure! We are lucky, senor."

"Hit it hard," Glendon said. "Take us up there, Manuel."

They rode behind the slender man, riding fast through the night, and Glendon knew that Buck's stubbornness was betraying him. Avery's letter had said, *Do your best to take him alive. The governor wants to make an example of him. If you cannot, shoot to kill.* Well, four men were dead and one captured, and it meant nothing. Only Buck counted, for as long as Buck rode free he would find more men of the same breed; and it would have to be done all over again. Glendon rode in the night and smelled pines as the trail lifted and began a twisting assault on the slopes; and Manuel was suddenly beside him, halting them all, saying,"Behind the big hill, senor. In the hollow."

"How far?"

"Half a mile, maybe."

"Get down," he said. "Tie the horses here. Form a line. Manuel, take us over."

They moved up the hill, off the trail, then on the sloping level of the side hill, then downward as the earth receded. Glendon smelled old fire smoke as they came to the edge of timber and felt grass under their boots. Manuel whispered, "Senor, they are in the cabin. Their horses are behind. Wait here."

They spread out in the trees facing the bottom of the hollow. Minutes later a man groaned and Buck's voice came clear and angry, "Get up, Ed. Get up and try!" Then came the sound of horses moving in the trees behind the cabin. Buck shouted and Glendon fired one barrel, then the other, shooting blind into the darkness below. He heard the cabin door slam shut, heard the cross bar drop in place, and only then did Glendon smile. Moments later he saw the tiny flame flicker, saw Manuel throwing wood on the cookfire, saw the cabin take shape in that light. Manuel ran then, carrying a lighted brand, around the back of the cabin, down on the north side; another fire started there and Glendon could see the door in those dancing flames. He almost laughed then; that was the end of Buck's last chance.

"Settle down," he said. "Watch that door. We'll wait it out."

He hitched himself around on the stony ground and raised the shotgun on the door and wished for a cigaret. Charley Leslie came crawling along and lay beside him, puffing from exertion.

"That man of yours is good," Glendon said.

"Plenty good," Leslie said. "Pat—"

"Yes?"

"You'd better understand something," Leslie said. "He works for Colter."

Glendon rolled on his side and wiped sweat from his eyes. A good deal that had puzzled him came clear: if Manuel was in Colter's pay and Leslie knew it, then that store—he could understand why Leslie had finally told him tonight. Colter wanted Buck dead, not on trial, and Manuel would be looking for the chance. But Leslie, in warning him, gave himself away. He would be watching two of them from now on.

"Thanks," he said. "I'll watch Manuel. I expect you to do the same. I want Buck alive."

"So do I," Charley Leslie said wickedly. "I want to see him hang."

Grey dawn came like a cripple running, lifting darkness from the hollow, showing the cabin beside the tank. They had waited out the night, Manuel had fed both fires, and no one had escaped the cabin. Glendon cleared his throat and called, "Buck?"

"That you, Pat?" Buck answered cheerfully.

"Give it up," Glendon said. "We know Bailey's hurt."

"Too early in the morning, Pat," Buck called. "Ain't got my boots on."

"Buck," he said. "You've got no chance."

"Oh, I don't know," Buck said. "We'll stick it a while, Pat. If you get nervous, come on down and get us."

"All right," Glendon spoke along the line. "Start working on that door, boys."

He watched the cabin take full shape as morning grew and the rifles began ripping into the door and the log chinks. He lay watching for an hour; and once the sun was up he stopped the firing and hailed the cabin again.

"Buck!"

"What now, Pat?"

"I've got no time to waste," Glendon said. "Open the door, throw your guns out. Walk out with your arms up."

"Pat, you're a stubborn cuss."

"Buck," he said coldly. "You're going to get hungry and thirsty. Bailey's hurt bad for all I know. I'm not waiting around all day. Take five minutes to make up your mind. Come out my way or we'll burn you out!"

Buck lay in the hole he had dug in the dirt floor. Ed Bailey was against the back wall with a dirty shirt sleeve tied around his shoulder. Ed grunted with pain and Buck said, "Shut up, you're not dead yet."

"You heard him," Bailey said. "He'll burn us out. We've got no chance."

Buck lay on his side and worked the hammer of his Colt, pulling back, releasing, staring at the riddled door. He knew there was no chance but it worried him no more than losing five men during the night. Time passed and finally Buck said, "You hungry, Ed?"

"I'm hurt," Bailey said. "Let's go in. We get another chance then."

"Sure," Buck said softly. "No jail holds me."

"Then tell him," Bailey said. "For God sakes, Buck. Tell him."

"Pat!"

"Yes," Glendon answered. "Five minutes are up."

"I'm hungry," Buck said. "Ed thinks he's dying. So I guess we'll give you this round. We're coming out."

Glendon called, "Watch the door," and trained his shotgun to the right where Manuel and Leslie were already standing in the tree shadows. Manuel glanced toward him, saw the shotgun, and lowered his rifle. Charley Leslie saw those twin muzzles, stepped back behind Manuel, and lifted one hand in agreement. Then the door was open, rifles and Colts flashed in the sunlight, arching through the doorway to the ground. When Buck stepped outside, supporting Ed Bailey, Glendon walked from the trees. Charley Leslie holstered his Colt, walked forward, and jerked Buck away from Ed Bailey.

"Burn my store," Leslie said. "I'll watch you dance for that, Buck."

"Let go," Glendon said curtly. "Manuel, take care of Bailey."

He took the handcuffs from his pocket, pinned Buck's hands behind his back, and snapped them on. He said quietly, "You all right, Buck?"

Buck was watching Manuel work over Ed Bailey. Buck looked around and smiled, and Glendon knew that Buck was grinning at the way Manuel lost his chance.

"Sure," Buck said. "Thanks, Pat."

"Don't thank me," Glendon said. "No prisoner of mine is manhandled. Jones, get the horses!"

Chapter Six

"I'VE BEEN SITTING HERE like a little girl in the dark," Swift said. "How did it really happen, Pat?"

They sat on the bench facing her garden in the cool August night that foretold fall weather, their first time together in three weeks. Glendon had spent those days at the capitol where the law's slow-grinding machinery moved toward the politically expedient conclusion. They were wanted in five counties, but the governor finally arranged to hold his prisoners' trial in the new Ellis County courthouse. Glendon had brought them home for tomorrow's trial, and now he sat relaxed for the first time in weeks.

"How?" he said. "Luck, the kind that kisses you once in a lifetime. That night we jumped them, Buck wouldn't listen to reason. Ed Bailey told me how he tried to warn Buck but they swung back on the cabin trail. Manuel smelled their dust and we followed them to the cabin. I used that trick once in the middle of summer in western Nebraska, so dry the dust was powder, hung in the air for hours. I trailed a man fifty miles; never saw him, caught him when his horse gave out. Dust and luck."

"What will happen to them?"

"Bailey and Buck will hang," Glendon said.

"Pat, how can you be sure?"

"McMillan is turning state's evidence," he said. "He'll testify that Buck shot and killed the telegraph operator, that Bailey killed a man on the Cross C last month."

"Judas," she said softly.

"What would you do?" Glendon asked. "He wants to live. The governor talked with him, knowing Buck might slip out if a clever lawyer took his case."

"But they rode together," Swift said. "Surely they had some feeling, some respect for each other."

"The governor talked to Ed Bailey," Glendon said. "He got nothing there. Bailey is the best man of the bunch."

"But how, Pat?"

"He's got a code," Glendon said. "Buck has none. Buck didn't give two cents for the men we killed. He forgot them the next day. He's talking with his lawyer tonight, Swift. Did you know that?"

"No."

"The smartest man in the territory," Glendon said. "Adams hired him, brought him down to defend Buck and Ed Bailey."

"Adams!"

"Don't ask me why," Glendon said wearily. "I could name a dozen reasons and each contradicts the others. But Adams put up the money and it'll be a fight . . . he thinks!"

"But won't it, Pat?"

"No," he said bluntly. "Not with McMillan. Nobody knows that but the governor, Avery, and me. I am telling you in confidence. Are you coming tomorrow?"

"I can't watch it," she said.

"Nobody wants to judge another," Glendon said. "It will always be that way. It should."

He stretched his arms stiffly against the darkness. He had lived on five hours' sleep a night for three weeks, and tomorrow would be a brutally long day. Swift rose beside him and looked toward the river; it was a windless night and the town behind them murmured with the expectant sound of people talking late. The hotel was jam-packed with newspaper men come hundreds of miles to watch the trial and report the results. A Roman carnival, in truth, for Buck was no longer a plain man. He was a legend one step from history, no matter that his last steps would take the gallows route.

"Late," he said. "Let's hope it begins and ends tomorrow."

"I've been thinking about us," she said timidly. "You told me to, remember?"

"Yes," he said. "I remember."

"If it ends tomorrow," she said, "what will you do?"

"Swift, I wish I knew," Glendon said. "Let's wait and see. Maybe we'll stay and maybe we won't, you and I. Let's hope for a vision."

"I need one," she said. "Stay or go, that's the question."

"Sleep on it," Glendon said gently. "Good-night, Swift."

When he entered the office next morning Leslie was back in the cell block, pursuing his favorite pastime of the last three weeks: giving Buck an unmerciful riding. Leslie spent a good share of his waking hours telling Buck exactly how much he'd enjoy watching Buck's heels dance in the air. Now, sitting at his desk, checking over the day's tight schedule, Glendon heard that cold voice telling Buck to shave, shine, and shampoo himself for the judge.

"Leslie!" he called.

Charley Leslie came from the cell block and offered Glendon a mock salute. He had waited weeks for today, and the triumph lay over his face in the smile and the curl of his lips.

"Charley," Glendon said, "stop playing the fool. You're getting under his skin and losing your sense of humor doing it."

"I'll not lose that," Leslie said. "I entertain no humorous thoughts about Buck"

"Lose your sense of humor," Glendon said, "and you're a gone goose. Everything turns sour, you end up chewing your own bile, wishing you were dead. Stop riding him. He'll be tried, convicted, and hung in a little while. What more do you want?"

"Anything I can get," Leslie said bitterly. "I'd like to spring the trap!"

"Because he won't whine?" Glendon said. "Because you can't break him, make him crawl, beg for mercy? Charley, you could ride him a year and he'd be tougher at the finish. Just don't give him a chance to do anything. Not one chance."

"I'd love that," Leslie said. "But he'll get no chance. As for the other, is that an order?"

"No order," he said. "I won't tell you how to talk and walk and live, Charley. Where's Jones?"

"Breakfast," Leslie said.

"I'm going out for a minute," Glendon said. "Now remember, when we bring them in, they come one at a time, ten feet apart, three of you on each man. During the trial you watch your own man every second."

"Don't worry," Leslie smiled. "They won't get foxy."

"Charley," he said, "you never know."

He left the office and went through the courtroom to the front steps. He stood in the morning sunshine and watched the crowd milling along the street and told himself to remember this day so it would not become distorted, so his memory would never tell lies if he lived long enough to enjoy memories. This was the last day of its kind these people would see in the territory. He saw the eager faces, heard the voices rising in a steady, expectant hum, a bee sound from one hive; he smelled the street and the horses at the rails, he saw the buggies and wagons, and he would not have been surprised if someone came limping up and asked where a man could buy cornplasters.

He looked once more at all the color and the cruelty, the wish for blood that lay shallowly buried in every man, and turned back into the courthouse to face a last distasteful job. He entered the cell block and stopped facing the first cell where McMillan sat in white-faced silence.

"Enough to eat?" he asked.

"Plenty," McMillan said tonelessly. "When do we start?"

"Few minutes," he said.

He moved on and faced Ed Bailey, saw the big man exercising the shoulder, almost healed now, with only a trace of stiffness in the torn muscles.

"Feel better?" he asked.

"Fine," Bailey said.

"Can I do anything for you?" he asked.

Ed Bailey looked around from the tiny window and cracked his lips in a narrow smile. Bailey respected him, and he in turn had respect for Bailey.

"I need a drink," Bailey said, "if it ain't against the court's wishes."

"In a minute," he said.

He went to the last cell in the corner, looked in upon the man lying in the bunk, wondered where the heart had gone, how the mouth could smile and the eyes crinkle, with a dead heart beating under that false face. For, as always, Buck smiled first and found the easy words.

"By God," Buck said, "you got yourself a night's sleep."

"Ten hours," he said. "I feel like a new man."

Buck swung off the bunk and came forward, gripped the bars in his manacled hands, and grinned. "Pat, where'd you get this steel?"

"Back East," he said. "Why?"

"I can't scratch it," Buck said. "Even if you sent me a file in a chocolate cake."

"No," he said. "You'd never make the grade, Buck. Want anything?"

"Nothing," Buck said. "When do we start?"

"Any minute," he said. He turned to include the other two in his next words. "Boys, don't try to walk too fast with those shackles on. Take your time going into the courtroom."

"I reckon they'll wait," Buck grinned. "An' we got us a smart lawyer, Pat. You watch out for fireworks."

"I've heard about him," Glendon said. "He's good."

He went quickly into his office, took the bottle from the bottom desk drawer, and returned to the cells. He uncorked the bottle and passed it to Ed Bailey, who drank shortly, wiped his lips, and said, "Many thanks, Glendon."

"McMillan?" he asked.

"Not now."

"Buck?"

"Roll me a smoke," Buck said.

He rolled a cigaret and passed it through the bars, held a match until Buck drew smoke and inhaled deeply. He saw the shadow on Buck's face, window shadow from the tiny east light, but it lay heavy as if a man might step into bright sunlight and still carry the cobweb grayness over his face.

"Good lawyer," Buck repeated, "but not good enough, eh?"

"No use lying," he said. "I doubt it, Buck."

He heard Leslie call, "Ready to go, Pat," and stood a moment, watching the boy who was older than most men. He walked into his office and faced his deputies. The newly appointed county clerk thrust his curly head through the outer door and said, "Sheriff, time to go," and before the door closed he heard the boot rumble of people crowding into the courtroom.

"All of you," he said curtly. 'Take your man. Keep watching him. McMillan goes first!"

The lawyer for the defense was a clever man who had no chance to show his mettle. Glendon never forgot the look on Buck's face when McMillan was called as a witness for the territory. McMillan took the stand and the prosecutor led him through a detailed description of the night Buck's gang rode down on the railroad telegraph stop, how Buck had shot the operator in cold blood; how Ed Bailey had backed Buck to the limit in that particular case and, in another, had fired the shot that killed a man on Cross C's southern range. Ed Bailey looked up in mild surprise at mention of that almost forgotten shooting; it was too late to do anything and the clever lawyer saw the truth. He did his best, but his best was useless. The evidence was presented to the jury, they withdrew for eight minutes by the clock, and returned with their verdict: "Guilty".

Glendon had stood behind his three prisoners, watching them, watching the courtroom behind the rail, noting the

presence of familiar faces among the sea of unknown eyes
and mouths and noses—Colter, Adams, Avery back there in
the shadow of anonymity—and heard Ed Bailey speak softly
in the utter silence, looking across the room at McMillan.

"You poor, spineless bastard!"

Buck never opened his mouth, just sat smiling faintly at
the jury, then at McMillan, as the next words came:

"The prisoners will rise and face the bench!"

Buck and Ed Bailey rose together; Glendon watched them
as the judge spoke the usual words, asking the prisoners if
they wished to make any statement as to why sentence should
not be passed upon them. They did not, and the judge,
conscious of the drama, cleared his throat and spoke first to
Ed Bailey.

"Edwin Bailey, I sentence you to be incarcerated in the
Ellis jail until September first, and on that date between
sunrise and sunset you will be hanged by the neck on a
gallows until you are dead!"

Ed Bailey met the judge's eyes squarely; and Glendon
knew that no one really cared what happened to Ed Bailey.
He was the frosting on the cake; he was the forgotten man.
They watched Buck and they waited for the words that came
now in measured tones:

"Buck Atherton, I sentence you to be incarcerated in the
Ellis jail until September first, and on that date between
sunrise and sunset you will be hanged by the neck on a
gallows until you are dead, dead, dead!"

"One week from today," Charley Leslie said. "Just seven
days, Buck. I hope you try something before then. I'm
disappointed."

Leslie stood facing the cell where lamplight shone weakly
on Buck's face. Leslie had eaten an hour ago, relieved Jones,
and waited now for Manuel Martinez to take over the night
guard. He had thrown bitter words at Buck for an hour, and
received nothing in return. When Manuel arrived Charley
Leslie said sourly, "So you've given up, eh?" and crossed
from the courthouse to the cafe, drank a cup of coffee, and
found his man waiting on the dark veranda.

"What a day," Adams said. "I'll never forget it, Charley."

"I noticed you sweating like a butcher," Leslie said. "What
did you think Buck might do?"

"If I was sweating," Adams smiled, "it was the heat, not
Buck. He'll do nothing with a dozen guards."

Charley Leslie had gained little satisfaction from Buck;

and now he had crossed the street to claim a promise made long weeks ago.

"I am resigning shortly," he said. "Eight days from now, to be exact."

"That is a shame," Adams said. "You've done a fine job, Charley."

"I'm not a deputy sheriff," Leslie said curtly. "I've developed richer tastes, C. B., and I'm too old to change. When do we start?"

"Start what, Charley?"

"You and I talked," Leslie said. "Some time ago. You dangled a proposition before my eyes, you suggested we discuss it at our leisure. I'll be at leisure in eight days and I expect a deal that fits my tastes."

"Of course," Adams said. "And I haven't forgotten. Will you take over the hotel?"

Charley Leslie threw his half-smoked cigar into the street. He began cursing softly and he continued to curse until his anger ran itself aground on his dry lips. He said then, "Don't joke with me. I want no hotel-clerk job, no saloon job, no cafe job, none of your penny-ante junk, Adams. You're in business again, and I want to be cut in."

"But I meant business," Adams said calmly. "Honest business. I'll do anything within reason—"

"How true," Leslie said. "Anything within reason. I can't name the page and verse but it'll be coming. Now for the last time—do you cut me in?"

"I'm sorry," Adams said. "I cannot offer you anything of that sort, Charley."

"You can't?"

"Nothing, Charley."

"Then I'm sorry too," Leslie said. "I just had a long talk with Buck. He still feels badly about the major's untimely death. He feels the major cheated him by dying and cutting off all that easy money. So he asked me what might happen if he wrote out a statement for the attorney general, or managed a meeting with that gentleman, and told him about you and the major, how he helped sell you so many hundred head of cattle. He remembers several hundred head they sold to you with blotted brands, so to speak, and rebranded with the major's brand, which, if I remember correctly, was not only registered in the major's name but in yours as well. Buck told me he can put his finger on fifty or sixty of those old hides. I told him to think it over three or four days and then let me know."

Charley Leslie lit a cigar and smiled above the match flare. He saw the round, red face whiten in sudden fear. "Well," Leslie said. "What should I do, C. B.?"

"All right," Adams said. "You've coppered my bet. What do you want?"

"I want to leave here," Leslie said, "with full pockets. What is it worth to make certain Buck never sees the attorney general, never writes a statement?"

"One thousand," Adams said without hesitation.

"I'm deaf, C. B."

"Two."

"I can't hear you."

"God damn you, Charley," Adams said. "I'll meet any price within reason. Name it."

"Five thousand," Leslie said. "Cash in advance."

"Half now," Adams said. "Half when the job's done."

"No," he said.

"Three and two, then."

"Stop it," Leslie said. "I'll take a turn up the street. Be upstairs when I come back, have the five thousand on your desk when I open the door. You've got ten minutes."

He strolled along the veranda, stepped down to the street, and walked past the courthouse. He smoked his cigar and smiled, thinking how the best of them finally came around when you touched the proper nerve. He had no intention of trying anything as stupid as shooting Buck in a cell and making it resemble a jail break. He returned to the hotel, went upstairs to the office that smelled of varnish and fresh paint, took the package of bills from the desk, and tipped his hat to the red-faced man in the swivel chair.

"When?" Adams said.

"Fifth or sixth day," Leslie said.

"No," Adams said. "No later than the fifth day."

"Agreed," Leslie said. "Watch for it, C. B. It'll be worth the price of admission . . . and you're the only man with a ticket, even if you will be sitting in a closed box."

He went downstairs and hurried through the town to Swift Stamm's house. He knocked and when she called, "Who is it?" he answered, "Charley," and entered the front room.

He stepped into the kitchen where coffee smell was fragrant and fresh cake was sliced on a white plate. Swift turned from the stove, motioned him to a chair, and said, "You're practically a stranger, Charley. Pat says you've done a wonderful job."

"Pat is very kind," Charley Leslie said. "I would like to

spend a good deal of time enumerating his attributes, but I'm here on business."

"Business, Charley?"

"Swift," he said, "we've been friends a long time."

"Yes," she said. "If it seems long to you."

"Roughly a year," Leslie said. "And a year here is a lifetime. Swift, what are your future plans?"

"For what?" she asked.

"Life, living—do you intend to go on alone forever?"

"There are worse ways," Swift Stamm said. "You seem to forget that I know most of them."

"And better," Leslie said. "Swift, this is in confidence. I'm leaving next week. I'm going to the Coast."

"I wish you luck, Charley."

"Swift!" Leslie said urgently. "Don't stay here and smother. I want you to come with me."

"Charley," she said lightly, "that's an indecent offer."

Leslie said, "I've never thought indecently of you, Swift. I want to marry you. How can I say it any better? Now wait, don't answer me now. Tell me in three or four days. I'm honest with you, so be honest with me."

"If you wish," Swift Stamm said gently. "But I'll tell you the same thing tonight or four nights from now."

"Glendon!" he said.

She turned to the stove and busied herself with the coffeepot while Charley Leslie absorbed a fact he had somehow missed in the past. He had not believed there was anything between them but friendship, and he still believed that was all. He knew that as he lived and breathed, and he could not understand how it had happened.

"Has he asked you?" he said.

"No."

"He won't," Leslie said quickly. "He's not your kind, he never will. He'll go his way and leave you alone. I've got hope now, Swift. I'll wait four days and whistle every hour. Good-night."

He went through the house into the darkness and did not hear her say, wonderingly, "Thank you, Charley. Thank you from the bottom of my heart."

Buck lay on his bunk and watched sun and darkness, the cycle of the days, pass his eyes. He did not look at McMillan once during those days, and he ignored Leslie as a man shuts out a minor irritant from his mind and body. On the morning of the sixth day Leslie just grinned at him, did not speak, and went away. Glendon came a few minutes later, checked every cell door, and was heard leaving the courthouse. Ed Bailey stood on his bunk, peered through the tiny cell window, and saw the workmen setting up the gallows.

"Getting the throne room ready," Bailey said.

"Good timber?" Buck asked.

"I reckon it'll hold us."

"Don't worry," Jones said from the door. "It'll hold both of you and room to spare."

"Always room for one more," Buck grinned. "Want to volunteer, Joe?"

"I'll fool 'em a while longer," Jones said, and turned into the office as other people entered. Buck heard Jones and the county clerk talking with C. B. Adams, telling Adams that Glendon had ridden north to meet Mr. Avery, who was coming down from the telegraph station, and was not expected back until late afternoon. The county clerk protested, Adams cited a dozen laws, and finally the clerk said, "Highly irregular but I can see no harm. You go along, Joe."

"Why, sure," Jones said. "Come on in, Mr. Adams."

Adams entered the cell block, stopped at Jones's command and submitted to a search. Adams said, "What is the meaning of this?" and Jones said sheepishly, "Orders, Mr. Adams. Nobody comes in here unless they're searched. You can stand outside Buck's cell but that's all. Sheriff's orders."

"Exactly my intentions," Adams said primly. "Now, if you don't mind."

He stepped around Jones, walked to the end cell where, his back to Jones, he winked twice and began talking quietly to Buck about the future. Listening, Jones heard C. B. Adams express concern over Buck's family, if any, and over any last wish or request Buck might have. Buck answered that he had no family and no last request except steak for breakfast. Adams talked on, thumbs in his vest, shaking his head sadly as Buck refused to act like a normal human being; and finally Buck said, "You mean well but what's the use. Go on back to your root beer, lawyer."

Adams had felt the doubt growing in him through the passing days, the feeling that at last he'd been taken lightly and politely. When nothing happened on the fifth day he knew he had to act. He did not doubt that Leslie had bilked him, but he doubted less that Buck might well sing a song tomorrow to the attorney general. Adams slept not at all that night, and reached his decision at breakfast.

He went upstairs, locked his door, and opened the safe. He removed the derringer, loaded in two fresh cartridges, and went over the tiny gun with an oiled rag. He slipped into his wide-sleeved black coat and attached the spring holder to his right forearm, just above the wrist. The derringer clamped in neatly, the shirt and coat sleeve hid the slight bulge. He took a fortifying drink from his private stock and walked steadily across the street to the courthouse. He won his argument, as he expected, and went down the aisle to the end cell. He winked twice and saw Buck's eyes narrow; and then he spoke on as only a lawyer could, until sufficient time had passed. Luck smiled just before he made his move.

The county clerk called to Jones, and C. B. Adams felt, rather than saw, the turning of Jones's head toward the office. He had the derringer in his hand by then. He wheeled, his right side to the cell, his body blocking a segment of bars and cell from view for the moment it took to start his turn. He tossed the derringer between the bars from that shortened distance of six inches, saw Buck's big hand engulf the gun; and then he was marching out of the cell block, through the courthouse, into the street.

He was trembling when he reached the hotel lobby, and he mastered that fear with great effort. He saw Charley Leslie at the cafe counter, drinking coffee, and that was more than enough to bring the thin smile to his face. He went upstairs and locked himself in his office. He placed the spring holder in the safe, removed his black coat, and rolled up his sleeves. He spread an inch-thick stack of legal papers on the desk, dipped his pen, and smudged his fingers with ink. Then he moved the big chair close to the windows, seated himself, and looked down upon the street. He could see the courthouse and most of the street. He tried to light a cigar but his fingers trembled the match into smoky blackness. He took another drink, corked the bottle, and settled back to wait. On the second try he lit the cigar and puffed in triumph.

"Now, Charley," C. B. Adams said aloud, "YOU get ready for the last act."

Buck palmed the derringer and stood motionless behind his cell door. McMillan was asleep, thank God, but Ed Bailey was already up and waiting, watching him in eager silence. Buck wasted no time pondering C. B. Adams' reason or motive; all he could see was freedom in the near distance . . . and squaring his debts before he left this place. Buck pawed at his shirt pocket for Durham and papers, pocketed the derringer, rolled a cigaret, slipped the derringer out and into his right hand, and held the cigaret ready in his left.

"Joe," he called.

"Now what?" Jones asked.

"Need a light," Buck said.

Jones said, "You must eat them matches," and came down the line, scratched a match on his pant seat, and extended it toward the bars. Waiting for the cigaret tip, Jones stared into the twin derringer muzzles leveled on his belt buckle.

"You got the keys?" Buck said.

Jones hesitated a split-second too long before he answered, "No!"

"I've got no time to fool," Buck said. "Lift that right arm above your head and yank those keys with your left."

Jones saw death in Buck's eyes. He wanted life desperately in that moment but he looked one last, hopeful time at the derringer and gauged his chances. Buck said softly, "I'll blow your belly out your back, Joe. Take a choice."

Up front, McMillan rolled over and grumbled in his sleep. He was coming awake and he'd yell his head off when he saw Buck with the derringer cocked and ready. Ed Bailey whispered, "Get 'em out, Joe!" and Jones took the key ring from his left hip pocket and inserted the proper key in Buck's cell lock. Then Buck was outside, spinning Jones around, jerking the Colt from his holster, tossing the derringer between the bars to Ed Bailey and following that with the key ring. Buck was five steps up the aisle when McMillan sat up and said, "What—?" and made a thin, throat-choked wordless sound.

"Shut up," Buck said genially. "Ed, you out?"

"Coming," Bailey said.

"Come on, Joe," Buck said. "Let's go make ourselves at home."

Bailey prodded Jones toward the office; and McMillan leaped on his bunk, grasped his window bars, and began shouting. McMillan had nothing to lose and he knew it too well. Back to his cell door, face pushed against his window bars, McMillan cried for help and waited for the shot. The county clerk came rushing from the courtroom, ran squarely into Buck's Colt, and fell in a faint to the floor. Bailey pushed Jones into the corner and backed off toward the gun rack, fumbled through the keys until his left hand, working blind, turned the padlock.

"Watch him," Bailey said.

Buck sat on one corner of the desk and grinned at Jones while Bailey rummaged through the stack, found his own

Colt and holster, found Buck's and tossed it onto the desk, then took two Winchesters and ammunition, closed the rack, snapped the lock, and pocketed the keys. McMillan was screaming now, a keening sound that carried down the street. Buck walked over to the inner door and smiled at McMillan.

"Turn around, Mac," Buck said.

McMillan wheeled from the window and took the first shot in the chest, the second shot in the face as he fell, tumbled off the bunk, and became a ragtaggle of clothes and flesh on the cell floor. Buck closed the cell block door, lifted Jones' double-barrel ten-gauge from the desk, and crossed the office to the courtroom door.

"Watch Joe for me," Buck said happily.

"Buck," Ed Bailey said, "let's move."

"I'm expecting a visitor," Buck smiled. "You just watch him."

Buck stood in the doorway, shotgun balanced against his hip, looking across the empty bench rows toward the hall doors. He heard boots thud up the steps, through the hall, and the door slammed back as Charley Leslie came charging down the center aisle. Buck let him come half a dozen steps, time enough to see the double barrel lift, to see Buck grinning at him above it. Buck had not been happy for weeks but this moment brought him nearer real joy than any he had ever felt; smiling, he pulled the trigger and watched the heavy buckshot load slam Charley Leslie against the benches. But not too soon; not before Leslie had seen him and had time—that second called eternity—to remember. Buck shuffled around the bailiff's table before the judge's bench and fired the other barrel into the body, raising dust puffs, bouncing the body on the floor.

"Buck!" Ed Bailey called. "Come on!"

Buck shuffled back into the office and grinned at Jones. "You stay where you are," he said. "Maybe you'll live longer. Ed, unlock these goddamn irons."

Bailey knelt down and unlocked Buck's leg irons, dropped the key ring, snatched it up, and worked with frenzied speed on the handcuffs. Buck drew his Colt and tossed the shotgun into a corner. Watching Jones, he took the Winchester and turned out of the office without a word, moving up the center aisle, over Leslie's body, through the hall into the bright sunlight on the courthouse steps. Behind him, Ed Bailey unlocked himself, scooped up the other Winchester, and prodded Jones into the cell block. He locked Jones in the first cell and ran stiff-legged to join Buck on the courthouse steps.

"Upstairs windows," Bailey said. "Don't stand here."

"Hell," Buck laughed, "we'll ride out. Nobody'll lift a finger."

Ed Bailey had no choice. He followed Buck down the street, jumped the first horse at the hotel hitch rail, kneed it sideways, tried to cover a dozen windows and doors. He cursed softly as Buck deliberately picked a good horse, and more deliberately rode it in a circle before the hotel. Ed Bailey would not understand the meaning or growth of a legend if someone painted such a picture under his eyes; but the truth came to him then, as they touched spurs and ran the length of the street toward the river, that no one in town dared aim a gun at Buck.

They crossed the river and passed the major's empty pens and raced for the hills; an hour later, pulling in for a blow, Bailey wiped his sweat-slick face and studied the back trail.

"Adams," he said hoarsely. "We owe him one, Buck."

"We owe him nothin'," Buck laughed. "Wanted us out of the country, the old bastard."

Bailey rubbed his bad shoulder and considered the unspent days and nights they faced. He had given up all hope that morning, had faced death and found himself equal to the task according to his own lights; and now he spoke words he had bottled up for months.

"We can get out if we use our heads."

"Damn," Buck said. "Not a match to my name."

"South," Ed Bailey said. "Get over the line and stay there."

"Compadre," Buck said, "you forgettin' we've rode together?"

"No," Bailey said. "I won't forget. You know that. But we're finished, Buck, an' I'm riding south."

Expecting the worst, Ed Bailey felt blessed relief when Buck fumbled for Durham and papers. Buck said, "Loan me a match."

Bailey gave him three and watched Buck light up and draw deeply. Buck looked down their back trail, tilted his hat, and smiled.

"You go on," Buck said. "I'll hang around a while."

"Buck," Bailey said, "that's the way Glendon'll figure you. Don't give him no advantage."

"Nobody pushes me," Buck said softly.

Ed Bailey swung his horse to the south and looked at Buck one last time. "I'll wait for you," he said. "Down below El Paso, south of the river."

"Don't wait too long," Buck said, and then his smile

vanished and the lips curled back. "Damn you, Ed. RIDE!"

All Glendon could do was sit in the office with Avery and Jones. Buck and Ed Bailey had a nine-hour start, and riding off half-cocked was simply a waste of time.

"They crossed the river," Glendon said. "Rode west. That's all we know." He held the derringer in his hand, jiggled it twice, and dropped it into a drawer. "We can cross Ed Bailey off. He won't stop until he's over the border. And he won't come back."

"But you think Buck will stay?" Avery asked.

"He'll stay."

"Which makes him a fool," Avery said.

"A fool," Glendon agreed, "and he can't tell you why himself. Call it pride, call it anything, maybe it has no name. But he'll stay. He'll hang around in the hills, along the river, duck into the sheep camps and try the town. Only it won't work out the same for him now, Avery. Those poor bastards were scared of him before; now they'll hate him. So he'll circle and double, and finally he'll head for Sherman. He was a king up there, he had that woman, he could walk the streets and not worry about getting shot. He'll come into Sherman sooner or later because, I think, he is looking for trouble; he wants us to ride his tail. We can sit back and let him alone, eventually get him, but we can't wait that long. The governor wants him fast, I can guess that. And if we give him time he might start thinking straight and do the logical thing—head for the border. Avery, how many men can you get in twenty-four hours?"

"Two hundred," Avery said. "Possibly more."

"Will you try my way?" Glendon said. "Push him hard and hope for a break?"

"I'm with you," Avery said. "You name it, Pat."

"Wire the governor," Glendon said. "Have every town watched. Start men pushing in toward Sherman from over in the Bravo valley, down from the railroad. Root into every sheep camp, cabin, ranch. Stop at the Cross C and ask Colter to throw his crew north and south along the Texas line and work this way. Can you get the governor to put up a reward for Buck? As big as he can make it."

"Five thousand," Avery said. "It will be five or more."

"Dead or alive," Glendon said. "But pass the word to shoot on sight. No use talking with him. He'll never come in alive."

"Where will you be?" Avery asked.

"Sherman," Glendon said. "I'll wait for him there."

"Pat," Jones said. "You got to take me with you. I can't stay in this country after today."

"Nobody blames you," Glendon said.

"Can I go?" Jones said thickly.

"Why, man," Glendon said, "you're the next sheriff of this county. I want you and Manuel. Go tell him."

He knew how Jones felt. To be on guard and let Buck escape was the worst possible punishment a good deputy could suffer; and Jones was becoming just that—a good man. He watched Jones run from the office, and heard Avery say, "You have an edifying effect on deputies, Pat."

"He came slow," Glendon said. "Just finding himself. He'll do."

"Now," Avery said briskly. "I'll be at the railroad in six hours. Give me until tomorrow night to put my men in motion. Do you want me to come down on Sherman?"

"Yes," he said, "but after dark. Then lay out to the north, east, and south, and don't cross the river to the west. I want Buck to come in that way without trouble, without suspicion. Jones and Manuel will be in the saloon. I'll be in that woman's house. I can't promise you anything, Avery. We might wait three days, we might sit three weeks. I'm hoping you can put enough pressure all around to push him in. Well, that's it."

"I'll see you at Sherman," Avery said. "Good luck."

Avery clapped on his hat and walked swiftly from the office. The county clerk hovered in the doorway and watched Glendon collect shotgun, ammunition, and small gear. When Glendon turned to go, the clerk said, "Sheriff, I'm ashamed of myself. I didn't do my duty this morning."

"Fainting?" Glendon said. "That was the luckiest thing you ever did."

"Lucky!"

"Yes," he said. "Are you married?"

"I am."

"Any children?"

"Not yet."

"Then you'll likely be a father some day," Glendon said. "If you hadn't fainted—"

"But he didn't shoot Joe," the clerk said.

"You never know," Glendon said quietly. "You never know why, or why not."

Leaving the courthouse, he met Jones and Manuel Martinez coming up the front steps. Manuel had taken charge of the bodies, made a list of effects, and now placed a grimy finger on one specific item: five thousand dollars safety-pinned inside Charley Leslie's shirt pocket.

"Lot of money," Manuel said. "Full of holes, all bloody."

"Where is it?" he asked.

"Clerk's office," Manuel said. "In the safe."

"All right," he said. "Meet me at the barn in ten minutes."

He walked down to the hotel and saw Adams behind the desk, bent studiously over the register. He crossed the lobby and stood silently against the desk until Adams looked up, smiled, and shook his head.

"A terrible business," Adams said. "I see you are going out. Good luck."

"Too bad about Charley," he said.

"My friend," Adams said solemnly. "I hope Buck suffers the tortures of hell. It was cold-blooded murder."

"I'll try to get to the bottom of it," Glendon said. "If I have time."

"Charley, you mean?"

"No," he said bluntly. "How Buck got that derringer."

"Derringer?" Adams said blankly. "Oh, was that the gun?"

"Buck left it on my desk," Glendon said. "And you were the last man to visit him."

"God above!" Adams said hollowly. "You don't believe—?"

"Charley had five thousand in cash on him," Glendon said. "He didn't own five hundred last week, he hadn't been out of town. Nobody here has that much money . . . nobody but one man. Charley got hold of five thousand dollars, Buck got hold of a derringer, but Charley didn't give it to him. I'll be doing some guessing while I'm gone. If I get back, I'll hang around until I figure it out. Maybe Buck'll have time to tell me."

"You are accusing me?" Adams said. "Accusing me of giving Buck that gun?"

"Not officially," Glendon said. "Just guessing."

"Just keep on with that crazy idea," Adams said hotly. "Just keep on with it, and I'll make you prove it, which you cannot. I know your kind, Glendon. You're grasping at straws to save your own hide. Well, let me tell you something, Glendon. You'll not use the legality of your office to bullyrag me."

"My office?" Glendon said softly. "I'm talking about you and me, Adams. Yes, I know my own kind. I'm not so different from Buck."

He went away from the hotel and through the sunny day

to his house. He saddled the big horse, strapped on his blanket roll, and headed for the gate; and Swift came running to catch his hand, then she was in his arms, head buried in his shoulder.

He said awkwardly, "I'm sorry as hell about Charley, Swift."

"You're going now?" she said.

"Got to," Glendon said. "Buck's way ahead."

"How long will you—?"

"I can't tell you that," he said. "Until it's over."

"Pat," she said. "Do you—I don't know how to say it. If you find Buck, what—?"

"There's a word for the way things stand," Glendon said. "Preaching is over. Buck won't be taken alive, Swift, if that's what you're trying to say. Will I shoot him? Swift, if I find him I'll kill him. Will I give him a break? No, there's nothing left between us. I don't believe in Robin Hood, Swift, I don't believe in fairy tales. I'll shoot him when I see him, front or back. That's my job and the sooner it's finished the sooner I can quit."

"Pat," she said. "I've got to ask you something."

"Yes?" he said, impatient now.

"Charley told me something the other night," she said. "He told me you would never ask me. I've been a damned fool and a coward to boot. Charley wanted me to go away with him. Then I knew what I wanted. I'm asking you, Pat. I don't care what you do, where you go. Will you take me?"

He swung the shotgun barrels away from her arm and touched her cheek with his rein hand. He said wonderingly, "You sure freckle up in the summertime," and then he pulled her close and they stood silently until the big horse jerked at the reins. Glendon said, "You wait right here, Swift. I'll do the asking."

Adams packed his bags with trembling fingers and told himself that Glendon could prove nothing, but he could not forget those words, "I'm not so different from Buck!" Adams understood those words too well. Buck took the law into his own hands, and Glendon had meant the same thing. Adams wondered how much he could realize from his new business; whatever it was, it was worth the loss to live again another day, a long way away. Opening his safe, stuffing the contents into a bag, he thought suddenly that Glendon had come last into their midst, and Glendon was the only man remaining.

"Fool," he said to the mirror above the safe. "You poor fool!"

Chapter Seven

BUCK RODE ALONE in a land he had ruled with the gun. Time without number he had ridden from night into the lonely sheep camps, off the timbered slopes into cabin yards, across flats to the aspen pole corrals where two-bit ranchers mustered up a half-fearful smile and dropped another steak in the pan. He knew all the towns tucked fairy-fashion amid the folded hills, he knew the rivers, he knew all the vast land where his gun was law. But he was not alone then; the others backed his play. He had ruled the land and awed its people; and now, one day and one night free, he sensed the change and felt the cold-wind warning of Ed Bailey's good-by.

He had dropped into a sheep camp southwest of Sherman that first night, ate mutton, talked with the mustached old herder and patted the dog that lay quiescent beside the piñon fire. The herder knew of his capture and sentence; and his presence meant only that he had escaped the gallows. The herder politely answered his questions, stuffed him with good mutton, but a fresh barrier lay between them when Buck rode away. He tried a western-pass trail leading over the mountains to the Bravo valley and, in early-morning high among the peaks, learned a caustic truth: the telegraph was faster than the best horse. He spotted the pass guards and ducked into timber as the long-range rifle shots sought him out. He turned back off the mountain trail and rode north. He ate his noonday meal in another sheep camp, sitting on a wagon tongue while the herder obeyed his commands and watched him with heavy-lidded eyes. Mounting, he gave the herder a cruel look.

"You wouldn't report me, eh?" he asked.

"Oh, no," the herder said. "Not you, Senor Buck."

"But you'd like to," Buck said.

"No senor."

"Then stick to your sheep," Buck said.

He rode north into thick timber along a ridge and watched the camp behind him in the valley. He saw the herder ride eastward toward the river; and that was the beginning of understanding. He was all alone; every hand had turned against him. For a moment he considered following the herder and settling another liar's account; but he had no time. He rode fast along the slopes until he came, in late afternoon, to the next canyon pass that wound westward over the mountains. He tried that pass and took a rifle slug through his hat, and ran his tiring horse far down into the lower timber before darkness covered him safely. Not that he was chased. Buck knew the difference between a serious pursuit and the old game of hazing a man until he dropped.

He slept in the timber and woke in early dawn with a loose belly. He watered the horse and drank deeply, and sat beneath an old bull pine, staring eastward across the plains. He had to get another horse, he wanted food and a drink, and he wanted a woman. He thought of Ed Bailey, by this time nearing the border, and he looked longingly toward Sherman, less than thirty miles to the northeast.

Buck dozed beneath the tree all day, sorting out his thoughts, thinking of Glendon and Colter and Adams—all the faces passed in review, old and young, dead and living. Some were smart, some dumb, and the smartest had died as easily as the bone-heads. McMann had called him a young fool, Adams had laughed at him behind his back, Colter had tried to use him and, failing, turned on him like a battle-scarred old cougar. Only Glendon had offered him honest friendship, treated him as an equal, and that was the worst part of it all. Pat was somewhere down there, ready to shoot on sight, probably staked out near Sherman, knowing damn well he'd try to sneak into town for a fresh horse, some grub, and a night with Juanita.

"All right," Buck said aloud. "One more time an' I'll listen to you, Ed."

One more time and he'd head south, cross the river, and join Ed Bailey. But first he'd go into Sherman, let everybody know they couldn't run him out of this country like a rabbit. Then he'd ride south and hold up his head. He relished that plan through the day, until the mountains cast lengthening shadows far across the plains; and rode the tired horse slowly off the slopes toward the river. He swung north and kept to the cottonwoods and the willows, followed the river bends, and dismounted in thick cottonwoods a mile below Sherman at eleven o'clock by his pocket watch. He tied the horse and waded the river, dried his feet and shoved on his boots; and walking into town heard the music and knew the day: Saturday, fandango night in Sherman. He grinned and rubbed his dirty jaw; he wasn't slicked up, he needed a shave, but be damned if he wouldn't look in on that dance.

Slipping along in the deep shadows, Buck reached the plaza. He could hear the music clearly, the laughter and singing and movement of people inside and out. He approached the barracks and looked through the south window, into the glare of the wall lamps shining yellow and smoking black. The music was loud and gay, the floor was covered with dancers, old folks crowded the benches, giggling girls filled the corners; but he did not see Juanita. He murmured, "Stayed home, by God!" and drew back from the window.

He circled far out into the empty plaza until he came abreast the saloon and saw the light in the windows. Coyote Smith always closed for the fandango; and he remembered he had seen Smith's wife at the dance but not the saloonkeeper. He went toward the saloon until he stood just outside the slanting window light. He saw Coyote Smith polishing glasses behind the bar . . . polishing over and over again, not talking, not pouring drinks, just moving a towel over the glasses. Then Smith came forward and moved between the lamplight and the window, giving Buck his first clear look deep inside. He saw a figure in the back corner, caught lamp glint on the shotgun, and recognized Jones. Buck grinned savagely and half-drew his Colt.

They already had the town staked out; and he'd bet there were men on the ridges and along the roads. He liked that; it made the game better. He circled far to the north and came down behind the saloon and closed in on Juanita's house. Moving through the weeds, guiding on the big cottonwood, he saw the faint lamplight in her east window. She stayed home from the fandango while Lopez was out in the hills. Fine, he'd take her down to the river and send her back later on for some grub and a fresh horse; and have her pass the word to Coyote Smith that he'd been a-callin. She'd want to go along. They always wanted to look over the hill, and they never realized that once they took up with him they were already looking far away. She was no different from the others.

Buck drew the Colt and stepped softly through the front

gate and came on to the front door. He stood against the wall beside the door and held the Colt on the ready.

"Nita," he whispered.

The house was silent to his call. He gave the door a push and it fell back, and lamplight flooded yellow over the graveled walk.

"Nita," he said. "Come out here!"

They rode all night and reached Sherman at eight o'clock next morning. While Manuel led the horses to the livery barn, Glendon entered the saloon and faced Coyote Smith. Jones was inspecting the other stores, covering his front, and Manuel would slip from the livery barn and come along the store backs.

Coyote Smith said, "You back again?" and pushed a bottle down the bar.

"Can we get breakfast?" Glendon asked.

"I'll tell the woman," Smith said gloomily.

Smith headed for the kitchen and Glendon said, "Call her!" Smith turned to protest, changed his mind, and called his wife; in that moment, as Glendon intended, Smith knew.

"We'll be here a while," Glendon said.

"How long?" Smith asked.

Glendon said, "Who cares, Smith?" and waited for Manuel and Jones. When they reported all clear he said, "We'll change off shifts. I'll take the house. Manuel, you move around. Jones, you'll headquarter in here. Now let's eat."

They took the back table and ate their breakfasts while Coyote Smith watched them warily. Glendon stepped out back and crossed the vacant lots to the Lopez house and met Lopez himself at the front gate, just about to leave with team and wagon. He saw the woman in the doorway, a shadowy figure, and placed one hand against Lopez's chest.

"You know me?" he asked.

"Yes, senor," Lopez said. "You are the sheriff."

"Go on about your business now," Glendon said. "But come back after dark and get your wife."

"My wife?"

"Get her out of here," Glendon said. "Don't let her out of your sight. Stay until you're broke, then come back."

He dropped five gold pieces into Lopez's hand and saw the dark face tighten in understanding. Lopez said softly, "He has escaped?"

"You can guess," Glendon said. "I can't tell you any more."

"Now I see," Lopez said. "Senor, I will take her away tonight. And I will pray for you."

"Pray for yourself," he said. "Don't worry about your house. I'll watch it."

He went through the gate, into the house, and faced the woman across the room. He saw in one glance why Buck came here, and came again. She had everything, and she had nothing; she had delicacy and she was hollow underneath. Glendon removed his hat and laid the shotgun on the table.

"Don't go out without my permission," he said. "I'll be here from now on."

"You cannot—!"

"Shut up!" he said wearily. "I want no trouble. Listen to me and we'll get along."

He settled himself in a chair that afforded him views through front and back doors. Juanita Lopez went to the front door and watched her husband drive away; and then the day commenced its slow unreeling. He sat out the morning, asking for coffee and drinking numberless cups, until Manuel came to stand guard while he slept. He woke in evening darkness and sent Manuel back to the saloon, and kept Juanita inside until Lopez returned.

Lopez ordered her to pack for a trip. She ran behind the table and sobbed her protest, and the sobbing became a scream; then Lopez struck her across the face, a blow that knocked her flat. He jerked her up, slapped her soundly, and spoke in Spanish that ripped and tore. She packed a sack docilely and walked in silence to the front door where Lopez grasped her arm and tipped his hat to Glendon.

"I am sorry," he said. "It was the only way."

"You've got horses?" Glendon asked.

"Good ones," Lopez said.

"Try Las Vegas," he said. "Above the railroad."

"I had Las Vegas in mind," Lopez said. "I have relatives there. Good luck, senor."

"And to you," he said.

Lopez led her from the house where Manuel waited to make sure she did not break and run; the horses walked away into the night and Manuel came to the front door.

"They are gone."

"I'll stick inside until midnight," Glendon said. "Then I'll be in the yard, on the north side."

"We are ready," Manuel said. "Good shooting!"

Manuel went away and he sat alone in the house that smelled and felt of Buck. He placed the lamp on the south wall shelf, turned the wick down low, and made himself comfortable behind the bed in the northwest corner of the room. He folded up a cushion of blankets and sat, back against the wall, with the shotgun across his knees. He listened to the night and thought of Buck, riding into nowhere.

At midnight he slipped outside with a blanket and squatted cross-legged beside the north yard fence. He felt ants moving in the sand under his legs, heard the chatter of night insects, the sound of horses and cows and goats in surrounding pens. Night lay high and thick, the stars were bright, then gray pennants lanced the sky and false dawn bloomed with a touch of dew-wet fall chill; and morning rose in the east.

He slept in a room behind the saloon while Manuel and Jones stood guard. He rose at noon and took over while they slept; toward suppertime a lone rider cantered into town and ordered a drink, glanced around at him, and winked. He motioned the rider over and said, "Nothing so far," and watched Coyote Smith absorb this byplay.

"Mr. Avery's all set," the rider said. "Any orders?"

"No," he said. "Just wait."

"Good luck," the rider said. "If you need us, we're primed and cocked. Passes are blocked, Colter's coming in from the east."

The rider rode away and Coyote Smith polished his glasses and ignored Glendon. Toward dark Manuel came up the back hall with Smith's wife and pushed her gently into the kitchen.

"She was saddling a horse," Manuel said. "I did not think she should ride on such a dark night, eh?"

"Bad for the bones," Glendon said. "Smith, don't try it again."

"Keep your hands off my woman," Smith said harshly.

"Keep your hands on the bar," Glendon said.

He slept an hour and woke to the boisterous talk of saloon customers awaiting the fandango. When he joined Jones at the back table, Smith requested permission to lock up during the dance. He said, "You stay here," and motioned Smith back to the bar. The crowd moved along to the barracks, the music began, and Glendon took the now familiar path to the Lopez house.

Settling in the corner, he wondered how long it might go on. He listened to the music and felt nothing special about the night. If Buck had changed his mind and followed Ed Bailey, he would look seven kinds of fool within the week.

He waited until midnight and prepared to move outside; and it came so swiftly he was caught on his knees, the shotgun pointing at the floor.

"Nita," Buck called.

Glendon had not laid his hammers down, the sheerest good luck, for he was cautious with the double barrel, uncocking it before he moved outside. He brought the shotgun up slowly until the butt pressed snugly into his shoulder and his heavy muscles corded inward and steadied the trembling barrels. He was on his knees in the half-darkness and the lamp shone boldly on the closed door; and then the door came open and released lamplight streamed thinly onto the hard-packed earth outside.

"Nita," Buck said. "Come out here!"

He couldn't speak and he could not shoot through three feet of adobe and touch Buck, who was flat against the wall beside the door. Buck had called twice, seeing the lamp, but he would not call again.

Glendon remembered his promise to Swift; to shoot back or front. And he knew, as he had always known, that he could not shoot any man in the back. He had carried the shotgun for years, but never had he shot a man in the back. He was a fraud to himself and had always been a fraud; and tonight he was no worse or better than ever in the past. When he needed ruthlessness, he thought of a man.

He sighted on the open doorway and waited; and heard a boot scuff the earth outside.

"Nita," Buck said softly. "If you're in there, sing out!"

His finger lay against the front trigger and the stock was sweaty hot on his cheek. He looked down the ramp between the barrels and watched the empty doorway. His breath was puffy on the stock, hot into his skin beneath the shirt. He heard the boot scuff again as Buck came away from the wall and faced the door, still hidden, the Colt hammer dropping and coming back to full cock with a sharp click. Buck was testing the Colt, listening to the silence.

"Pat," Buck said, "you fooled me good. I know you're in there."

He held his breath, watching the door, waiting for sound of advance or retreat; for Buck had to make a play or run for the river. If he spoke it would do no good, it would change nothing. He opened his left hand under the forearm and brought the fingers back hard and tight around the checkered wood, and waited in silence.

"Pat," Buck said again, "I know you're in there, God damn you! Come on out, Pat."

He waited and the silence became a brass band, cymballing all the past through his ears: Buck at the Cross C cookhouse table, lazying over coffee; Buck in town, buying the drinks for a new friend with his last four-bits, laughing. He waited in the silent darkness; and he knew, as Buck knew, that it could not last much longer.

"All right, Pat," Buck said. "I can't get in and you can't get out. Guess I'll have to leave you. Pat, I reckon you'd appreciate knowing—Adams slipped me that derringer."

He ignored those last words, listening closely, for the boots scuffed on the earth as Buck slipped backward around the corner of the house. Glendon came off his knees in his socked feet and ran straight through the front door and around to the north toward the fence. He had left the back door open and lamplight shone for the distance of a man's height on the backyard. He moved along the fence, cleared the house, and saw the back door and that thin slice of brown earth. He went down on his belly and cradled the shotgun; and heard, faintly, the boots at the southwest corner beyond the open door.

"Hell," Buck called. "You better come out if you want a last chance, Pat. I ain't goin' to stay all night."

No, he thought, but you've got to do something, Buck. Break for the river, go uptown, go somewhere. Manuel's prowling the night and you'll never know when he might bust it wide open with that handmade torch of his. Buck stood fast at the corner; and from the south, out on the street, Manuel Martinez called:

"Sheriff!"

He did not answer and felt the seconds running icy through his mind, and then Manuel shouted, "I understand, Sheriff."

He waited, watching the doorway and the invisible corner beyond; and the torch was a streak in the sky, lit and thrown toward the house from the street, orange-red and flaming, throwing sparks, arching high and falling behind the house to light up all that side. Manuel shouted, "ALTO!" and the Winchester tore the silence apart.

He saw Buck appear, silhouetted against the torch light, moving north, a black shadow against the wall as he leaped from the orange-red light. Buck poised there for one endless moment, then came on north through the doorway light; and he saw the shirt front take shape in his front sight and called out, against all his will:

"Buck, give up!"

There was no gap between his last word and the first shot. Buck whirled and came running, the Colt aflame, the slugs tearing into the dirt all around Glendon; and he pressed the front trigger and felt the brutal recoil of the ten-gauge, and pressed the back trigger without volition, and lay in the night on the hard earth and knew he was crying. Not for Buck, he had no tears for Buck, but for what a man must do to live.

Head down on the stock, he cried silently and then he heard the running feet and found himself erect, walking forward, meeting Manuel Martinez across the legend in the dust.